and the Journey to Toog

Poog

Gax

Akiko

Mr. Beeba

Spuckler

and the Journey to Toog

Written and illustrated by

MARK CRILLEY

JPap

JAMES PRENDERGAST LIBRARY ASSOCIATION

04913774

A Yearling Book

Published by
Yearling
an imprint of
Random House Children's Books
a division of Random House, Inc.
New York

If you purchased this book without a cover you should be aware that this book
is stolen property. It was reported as "unsold and destroyed" to the publisher
and neither the author nor the publisher has received any payment for this
"stripped book."

Copyright © 2003 by Mark Crilley

Akiko, Spuckler Boach, Poog, Mr. Beeba, Gax, and all other characters
contained within, their likenesses and other indicia are trademark Sirius
Entertainment, Inc. All rights reserved.

All rights reserved. No part of this book may be reproduced or transmitted in
any form or by any means, electronic or mechanical, including photocopying,
recording, or by any information storage and retrieval system, without the
written permission of the publisher, except where permitted by law.
For information address Delacorte Press.

Yearling and the jumping horse design are registered trademarks of
Random House, Inc.

Visit us on the Web! www.randomhouse.com/kids

Educators and librarians, for a variety of teaching tools, visit us at
www.randomhouse.com/teachers

ISBN: 0-440-41893-3

Reprinted by arrangement with Delacorte Press

Printed in the United States of America

September 2005

10 9 8 7 6 5 4 3 2 1

OPM

To Conrad Hilberry,
who taught me about words,
and David Small,
who taught me about pictures

ACKNOWLEDGMENTS

Thanks to all the Akiko readers who have demanded "More Poog! More Poog!" over the years. I might never have gotten around to this story if not for you. Thanks to my editor Jennifer Wingertzahn, who helped me write about a character who has no arms and no legs and who speaks a language even *I* don't understand. A special thank-you to my new book designer, Marci Senders, who is truly a joy to work with. Thanks also to Colleen Fellingham, Emily Jacobs, Channing Saltonstall, and Ashley Caro. And, as always, hugs and kisses to my wife, Miki, and son, Matthew (who is now old enough to draw lovely Poogs of his own).

Chapter 1

My name is Akiko. I'm a pretty average fifth grader in a pretty average town that's right in the middle of a pretty average part of the country. My life is for the most part extremely dull. For the most part. It's the *least* part that's always getting me into trouble. The part that has to do with me being taken off to other galaxies, battling strange aliens, piloting rocket ships, and, on occasion, eating in intergalactic fast-food restaurants.

People are always telling me not to exaggerate. Which bugs me because I never do. It's just that the things that happen to me tend to happen in a pretty big way. So please don't think I'm exaggerating when I say that the story I'm going to tell you right now is basically about the end of the world. Well, the end of *a* world, anyway.

Or a world that *nearly* came to an end. *Very* nearly.

Maybe I'd better just tell the story.

It all started on my way home from school.

I had just gone into Chuck's. Chuck's is this convenience store about three blocks from Middleton Elementary. It doesn't look like much from the outside, but it has the biggest supply of bubble gum in town. All the usual gums, of course, but the rare stuff too: Arkey Malarkey's Rain-Bo Day-Glo Sparkle Gum. Captain Zack's Holy Mackerel Rub-A-Dubble Gum. Even Abe & Mabel's Pop-N-Ploppin Super-Supple Bupple-Gum (That's right: *Bupple*). The gum I bought that day was something I'd never tried before. It was called Dr. Yubble's Ooey-Gooey Double-Trouble Bubble Gum.

I gave Chuck his money and got my nickel in change. Then I stepped out onto the corner, pulled out a piece of gum, unwrapped it, popped it in my mouth, and chewed.

So was it double trouble?

Not really. It was gooey. And ooey. *Definitely* ooey. But to call it trouble? I don't know. That's going too far.

Oh well, I thought. At least it's ooey. That's hard to come by in a gum.

2

So there I was, chewing gum, standing on the corner of Wabash and Fifth. The light changed and I began to cross the street. But before I got even halfway . . .

BUH-WOOOOOOOOOOooooooooo

A siren! I spun around and found a black-and-white car barreling down the street at me, its siren blasting, its tires weaving back and forth. It squealed to a halt just inches from my legs.

They're pulling me over? For *what*?

I looked around to see if anyone was watching; the last thing I needed was a bunch of gawkers crowding in to see what was going on. I was lucky. The only witnesses were a grandma and her cat peering down from a third-story window across the street, and a grocer, half a block away, squinting from the shade of his awning.

I turned back to face the patrol car. I'd never been so close to one before. The words MIDDLETON POLICE were painted on the hood, black on white. On the roof of the car was not one but eight flashing lights, each spinning and strobing a different color. Smoke billowed out in all directions, delivering a stink like an airport runway, only worse.

This was one *weird* police car.

The siren stopped.

KLAKKA-K'CHAK!

A door popped open in the middle of the hood, and out came a small mechanized megaphone. It could have come from a sci-fi movie, except it looked more like a sixth grader's homemade science project. It rose into a position between me and the windshield and rotated until it was pointed directly at my head.

A crackle of static, then:

"Please step over to the door of the vehicle, Aki—"

A pause.

"—er, little girl."

I took a few steps toward the driver's side of the car.

Aki—? Whoever was manning that megaphone had started to say my name. And he sure didn't sound like a policeman. He sounded an awful lot like . . .

"Not *that* door." A cough. "The other one."

I stopped in my tracks, reversed direction, and walked to the passenger's side of the car. There was a muffled *whump* and all the lights on the roof went out. Then they flashed on again. Finally there was a louder *whump* and they went out for good.

This was *not* the Middleton Police.

The passenger-seat window went down, and there before me was Mr. Beeba. He was dressed in his usual brown space suit and oversized yellow gloves but was wearing dark glasses for some reason.

"Quickly, Akiko!" he whispered, the words coming from both his mouth and the megaphone. "Into the backseat!"

"Shut off the dagnabbed speaker thing, will ya,

5

Beebs?" Spuckler Boach was at the wheel, unshaven chin, scraggly blue hair, and all. "You're whisperin' to the whole dang neighborhood!" Mr. Beeba twisted a knob on the dashboard and with great effort managed to get the megaphone switched off and back under the hood. Through the open window I could just make out the silhouette of Gax in the backseat, his robot head quivering nervously on his long, spindly neck.

"HELLO, MA'AM," he said.

"Quickly!" Mr. Beeba said again, this time without the echo of the megaphone.

It's funny. Seeing my friends from the planet Smoo hiding in a police car was one of the silliest things I'd ever laid eyes on. They just looked so *ridiculous.* But something told me—the expressions on their faces, mostly—that this was no laughing matter.

"*Please,* Akiko." Mr. Beeba's brow was furrowed into several chunky wrinkles. "Time is of the essence. We'll explain later."

These guys. They always explained later.

"Now, hang on a second," I said. "This, uh . . ." I waved a hand in front of me. "This isn't a real police car."

Mr. Beeba adjusted his dark glasses. "It's not *only* a police car, no."

I narrowed my eyes.

"It's a spaceship, isn't it?"

He and Spuckler both nodded.

I took another long look at the boxy black-and-white car parked in front of me. It was hard to believe this thing had just rocketed through a half-dozen distant galaxies before landing near the corner of Wabash and Fifth.

"There ain't no time for chitchat, 'Kiko," Spuckler said, pulling a knob that popped open the back door on my side of the car. "Trust me, you gotta come with us. Right now."

I looked across the street and down the block. Both grandma and cat had gone inside their apartment, and the grocer was busily rearranging a pyramid of grapefruits with his back turned to me. No one would notice a thing. But . . .

"Guys, guys, guys. We've got to make some rules here. This whole zooming-into-Middleton-c'mon-Akiko-let's-go thing is really starting to get on my nerves."

"It's Poog," Mr. Beeba said.

Poog. I leaned over to get a better view of the car's interior. My round, purple floating friend was nowhere to be seen.

"He's in trouble." Mr. Beeba took off his dark glasses, revealing panicked eyes. "Grave, grave trouble."

Poog? In trouble?

That changed *everything*.

I shook my backpack off my shoulders as quickly as I could and scrambled into the back of the car, slamming the door behind me. Spuckler and Mr. Beeba smiled from the front seat, both visibly relieved.

"What are you *waiting* for?" I said. "Poog's in trouble. *Go!*"

Chapter 2

I'd almost forgotten the most important part of leaving Earth: the replacement robot.

"Where is she?" I asked as Spuckler pulled into a nearby alleyway.

"In the trunk." He stopped and yanked a lever. There was a loud *wunk* directly behind me.

"The *trunk*? You've had my replacement robot trapped back there all this time?"

"She's a robot, Akiko," Mr. Beeba explained. "Robots don't mind being locked in trunks. They're very used to that sort of thing, I assure you."

"TYPICAL," Gax said with an indignant squeak.

A moment later I was looking at myself—or a pretty good copy of me, anyway—standing outside the car. She had the exact same clothes as me, the same pig-tails, everything.

dunk dunk dunk

She was knocking on the glass.

"Yes?" Mr. Beeba lowered the window nearest me. "What is it?"

"The backpack," said the Akiko robot. "I'll be needing that."

"Oh jeez, yeah," I said, handing it to her. "Good luck! I'll be back, uh . . ."

I looked questioningly at Mr. Beeba. He shrugged.

". . . whenever."

I fastened my seat belt and watched as the Akiko robot trotted back to Wabash Avenue and continued my walk home.

"All righty, folks," Spuckler said, "hold on to your heinies!" He hammered a button on the dashboard: The entire car noisily hoisted itself upright like a dog rising on its haunches. Soon the hood was pointed straight up at the sky and we were all flat on our backs, feet in the air.

Spuckler revved the engines and the car began to lift off. "Say goodbye to planet Orth!"

"Earth!" I shouted, but I'm pretty sure he didn't hear me.

The walls of the alley blurred and zipped away as we shot up over the rooftops. The car filled with sunlight. Middleton and the countryside around it twirled off beneath the clouds. Within seconds we passed through the upper reaches of the atmosphere and rocketed out into the stars. Peering through the back window, I watched the blue-and-green circle of Earth shrink, shrink, shrink and finally vanish altogether.

I slumped into the cushions of the backseat. All right. Time to find out what was going on.

"What sort of trouble is Poog in?"

Mr. Beeba turned to me from the front seat. "We're not exactly sure. As with so many matters pertaining to Poog, it's all a bit of a mystery, I'm afraid."

"Oh, come on. You must know *something*."

"Yes, well, a few days ago Poog received an urgent distress call from his home planet. . . ."

"Toog?"

"Ah, you remember." Mr. Beeba tapped a finger on his temple. "That's a real gem of a brain you've got there, Akiko. Such a shame you're frittering it away at Middleton Elementary. When are you going to start pursuing a master's degree, that's what I'd like to know."

"Yeah, yeah, yeah." Only Mr. Beeba could go off on a tangent at a time like this. I turned to Spuckler. "So Poog got a distress call from the planet Toog. Then what?"

"Well, he kinda flipped out, 'Kiko," Spuckler said, turning to shoot a glance at me, "which—you know Poog—ain't somethin' he does too often."

"Flipped out?"

"Oh yeah, he was practically bouncin' his little purple self off the walls, yammerin' away about how the whole darn planet was in a world of hurt. So he took off for Toog all by himself, jus' as fast as his legs would carry him. If he *had* legs. You get what I mean."

"You guys let him go there all alone?" I asked. "When the whole *planet* was in danger? What are you, nuts?"

"WE HAD NO CHOICE, MA'AM," Gax said. "HE *INSISTED* ON US NOT JOINING HIM."

"Really? That's weird."

"Oh, but it isn't, Akiko," Mr. Beeba said. "The inhabitants of Toog believe their planet is very sacred—one of the universe's holiest places, in fact. It is a violation of their principles for any non-Toogolian to set foot on its surface."

"So where are we going right now?"

Mr. Beeba's mouth curled into a half smile. "Why, Toog, of course."

I looked at Mr. Beeba, then Spuckler, then Gax.

"I take it we're about to violate some sacred principles."

Spuckler spun all the way around. "Well, what th' heck *else* are we s'posed to do? Here Poog goes hightailin' it off into the thick of danger, tellin' us he'll be right back an' everything'll be just fine 'n' dandy. Then we don't hear a peep out of him for three solid days."

"Clearly something has gone wrong," Mr. Beeba said. "Much as I hate to desecrate holy ground, I'm afraid we've got to find Poog and make sure he's not been hurt."

I stared out the window at the sea of stars flowing by. "A whole planet in trouble, eh? I wonder what the problem is."

"Your guess is as good as mine, Akiko," Mr. Beeba said. He paused, then added: "Well, very *nearly* as good as mine, at any rate."

"Do we even know how we're going to *find* Poog once we get there?"

"Nope," Spuckler said.

I was beginning to get a very bad feeling about this whole situation. We were heading to a planet none of us had ever been to before—a place where we were apparently not the least bit welcome—to deal with some sort of terrible threat that we knew absolutely nothing about. It sounded like an excellent recipe for total disaster.

But one thing was clear: Poog was in trouble. And if Poog was in trouble, I wanted to be right there in trouble with him.

Chapter 3

An hour or so passed. The more I thought about Poog, the more I realized how little I knew about him. He was such an important part of our team, but I could hardly tell you anything about his past, his likes and dislikes, or even if he had any family. After all the adventures we'd been on together, and even though I felt some sort of special . . . I don't know, *connection* with him, I had to admit I knew practically nothing about what was hidden behind that round purple face and those shiny black eyes.

Finally the planet Toog came into view. It was a tiny thing, probably a tenth the size of Earth, completely hidden beneath a white shield of cloud cover. As we circled

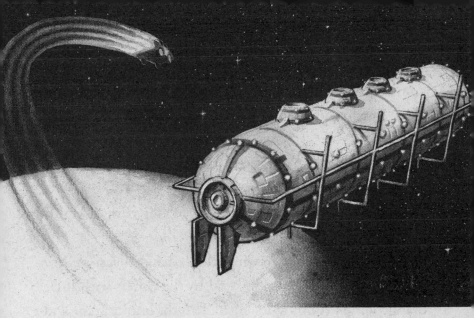

it, we came upon something tucked away on the other side: a gigantic space tanker, yellow with black trim.

"An interstellar transport cruiser," Mr. Beeba said. "That's odd. *Decidedly* odd."

I leaned over to get a better look. "What's so odd about it?"

"Ships of this sort are used mainly for transgalactic irrigation, Akiko; they move huge quantities of water from overly wet planets to overly dry ones. I don't recall Poog ever saying that his home planet had an excess of water. Or a paucity of it, for that matter."

"Paw-city?" I asked.

"*Paucity*. A very important word, Akiko. You should

commit it to memory and use it in conversation as often as you can. Think of it as the opposite of surfeit."

"Surf-it?"

"Really, Akiko. You must start carrying a dictionary around with you."

"Don't listen to him, 'Kiko," Spuckler said. "Dictionaries're for sissies."

We were steadily moving closer to the vast yellow ship. It was miles from one end to the other, with little orange lamps running its entire length, blinking on and off like lights on a radio tower.

"Better not get any closer, Spuckler," Mr. Beeba warned. "We have no idea whether this is a friend or a foe."

"Sure we do," Spuckler said. "It's a foe."

Mr. Beeba's face shivered in disbelief. "Then why in heaven's name are you heading directly *toward* it?"

"Beeba, we're talkin' about an irrigation ship. What's it gonna do, squirt water on us?"

"I'M AFRAID I MUST CONCUR WITH MR. BEEBA, SIR," Gax said. "TRANSPORT SHIPS OF THIS SORT, THOUGH GENERALLY UNARMED, ARE SOMETIMES ACCOMPANIED BY . . ."

FLOOOOOM!

Something shot by us on the left, filling the cabin with a flash of blinding white light.

"... DEFENSE MECHANISMS."

"Wh-what was that?" I asked, whirling my head to follow the path of the object.

"See whatcha done, Beebs? Ya got 'Kiko so nervous she's jumpin' at her own shadow."

"She's not jumping at *shadows,* you nincompoop!" Mr. Beeba growled. "She's jumping at *that!*"

A white orb of light, hundreds of yards away, was carving a silent arc through the stars, circling back toward us.

"Well, I'll be jiminy-jiggered," Spuckler said. "A spolarian drobe mine. One of them new heat-seekin' models."

"Don't just sit there *admiring* the thing, you fool! Get us *out* of here!"

Spuckler took both his hands off the wheel and sighed. "Look. Who's flyin' this ship? *You?*"

"Spuckler!" I cried. "It's going to hit us!"

The glowing white orb grew larger and larger. You could actually hear it rocketing through space.

sssssssshhhhh

"Look, 'Kiko, I know you're in the fifth grade an' everything." Spuckler put one hand on the steering wheel and rested the other on the dashboard. "But don't you think I know a *little* bit more about spolarian drobe mines than you do?"

Mr. Beeba was stabbing at the window with his fingers, gasping for air. "It's . . . it's . . . it's . . ." He never did manage to complete the sentence.

SSSSSSSSHHHHH

"THREE SECONDS TO IMPACT, SIR," Gax said.

The cabin filled with white-hot light. I braced myself for the blow.

SSSSSSSSSSSHHHHHHHHH

"TWO SECONDS."

SSSSSSSSSSSSSSSHHHHHHHHHHHH

"ONE SECOND . . ."

ZOOOOOOSSSSHHHH!

We dropped at top speed, like a roller coaster off its steepest hill. My stomach felt as if it had leaped into my lungs—my *head*, even. Mr. Beeba's face was smooshed up against the ceiling, surrounded by several of Gax's spare parts, which were plastered into position as if they'd been glued there.

"Whaa-HOOOOOH!" cried Spuckler. He finally punched a few buttons on the dashboard, abruptly slowing our fall. My stomach relocated to somewhere down around my knees.

"That's whatcha call the death drop. What *I* call it, anyway. It's the only surefire way of dodgin' a heat seeker."

"You idiot!" Mr. Beeba's legs poked up from the front seat, his head probably not too far from Spuckler's feet. "You're a lunatic! A *lunatic*, I say!"

"Beebs, you got a mighty funny way of showin' your gratitude."

"IT'S COMING BACK FOR ANOTHER GO AT US, SIR," Gax said.

Sure enough, the white-hot fireball was already turning around.

"Dagnabbit," grumbled Spuckler. "The li'l upstart don't know when to leave well enough alone."

This time Spuckler began flying straight toward the big yellow space tanker. He eased up on the speed a bit, allowing the drobe mine to come after us like a dog chasing a truck.

ffffffffffffff

"Now, this one I call the old bait 'n' switch," Spuckler

explained. "Ya get the little sucker hot on your heels . . ."

Mr. Beeba had stopped protesting. He was just whimpering and rocking back and forth in the front seat.

". . . an' ya start flyin' fast as ya can, straight at something real big an' hard. . . ."

FFFFFFFFFFFFFFF

The yellow tanker's steely surface shimmered in the starlight.

". . . This here transport cruiser, for instance . . ."

FFFFFFFFFFFFFFFFFFFFFF

The drobe mine was gaining on us. Its heat was burning the back of my neck.

". . . an' then at the last possible second . . ."

FFFFFFFFFFFFFFFFFFFFFFFFFFFF

The space tanker. The drobe mine. It was between crashing into one and getting crashed into by the other. I threw my head into my hands and tried to roll up into a ball.

". . . ya change course!"

SSSHHHEEEEEEWWWWWW

Our ship rocketed upward, rotated sideways, and shot between two enormous girders jutting out from the top of the tanker. We must have cleared them by a matter of inches.

FFFFLLOOOOOOOOOOOMMMM!

The drobe mine exploded in a ball of red-orange flame as it slammed into one of the girders. We zoomed out into the stars, our ship shuddering as if it, too, were slightly amazed to still be in one piece.

I peered over the front seat and saw that Mr. Beeba had fainted.

"All right, enough sight-seein'," Spuckler said. "Let's go down and find out what's cookin' on Toog."

Chapter 4

Soon we were deep within the overcast skies of Toog. The clouds came in layers, each a slightly different shade and thickness from the ones above and below. Our ship plunged through them like a submarine diving to the bottom of a vast white ocean. Occasionally we would emerge from the mist and catch a glimpse of the pale purple sky, only to drop into another layer of clouds and be blinded again.

Gax kept making announcements, assuring us that there was indeed a planet somewhere underneath all this. Mr. Beeba—who had awoken from his fainting spell in a very foul mood—limited himself to a few mumbled gripes about Spuckler's "devil-may-care exploits" and "wanton disregard for the safety of the crew."

The ship grew colder. My breath came out in misty puffs, and I had to keep wiping peepholes in the windows to give myself a chance of seeing anything. Judging by the temperature, I figured we'd get to the bottom of the clouds and find nothing but snow and ice.

"LAND HO," Gax said. "WE WILL REACH THE SURFACE IN APPROXIMATELY SEVENTEEN SECONDS."

I wiped a fresh peephole in the glass and prepared to get my first look at the planet Toog. But Toog kept me waiting: The clouds were thicker than ever.

"You sure about that, ol' buddy?" Spuckler said, fiddling with dials on the dashboard. "I can't see a dad-burned—"

FFWWAAAAMM!

We struck something. Hard.

THWUUUK!

The whole ship flipped sideways . . .

KLAAAAM!

. . . then upside down . . .

THRUMP!

. . . then began to roll.

FWUT-FWUT-FWUT-FWUT-FWUT-FWUT

I tried to keep my eyes open, but all I saw was a jumbled blur of whites and grays. Objects crashed into me, I crashed into Gax, and both of us crashed into everything else in the ship as we rolled, rolled, rolled. . . .

BA-CHUNT

    BA-CHUNT

        BA-CHUNT

Finally . . .

    . . . slowly . . .

        . . . bit by bit . . .

            . . . the ship . . . came . . . to a stop.

We were somewhere between sideways and upside down. A gust of wind whistled outside. Snow speckled the windows.

Spuckler was the first to speak.

"Sorry 'bout that, gang. Ever'body still alive?"

"I'm okay," I said, struggling to get myself upright.

"Good, 'Kiko, good. How 'bout you, Gax?"

"STILL FUNCTIONING NORMALLY, SIR, SO FAR AS I CAN TELL."

"Beebs?"

There was a grunting noise.

"You're gonna have to speak up, Beebs. I can't hear a thing you're sayin'."

"I said," Mr. Beeba said, his voice still quite muffled, "that I'd be feeling a lot better if you weren't SITTING ON MY HEAD!"

"Oh!" Spuckler jerked his body around, prompting further groans from Mr. Beeba. "Sorry 'bout that." Several *Ouch*es and *You idiot*s later, Spuckler and Mr. Beeba finally managed to free themselves of each other.

After a brief discussion about what to do next, we all agreed it would be best to get out and have a look around.

So we got out.

And had a look around.

We were in a snow-covered valley, surrounded by walls of ice that rose hundreds of feet into the sky. It was surprisingly warm for a place that looked so much like Antarctica. Apart from a wide white gash created by our ship, the surface of the snow was unbroken as far as the eye could see. It absorbed every sound we made, leaving nothing but the soft blowing of the wind.

Mr. Beeba cleared his throat. "I know this isn't going to make me very popular, but I'm afraid I must insist that we leave the ship behind. The rest of the journey will have to be on foot."

Spuckler spun around, his eyes bulging. "On *foot*? What are ya, crazy?"

"The inhabitants of Toog are highly suspicious of advanced technology. They are ascetics, and as such will look upon us with extreme disfavor if we go rocketing about their planet like a bunch of hot-rodders."

"Beebs," Spuckler said, "we're here to help *save* these fellers. If they don't like the way we get around, that's just their tough luck. Beggars can't be choosers."

"This is not a matter for debate," Mr. Beeba said, folding his arms.

I stepped between the two of them. "Spuckler, I think Mr. Beeba's right. We're already breaking one of their rules just by *being* here. We shouldn't push our luck by breaking two of their rules at once."

"Rules," grumbled Spuckler before making a face and spitting in the snow. He went over to the ship and bid it farewell. "We'll be back for ya. You jus' sit tight."

With our movement limited to where we could go on foot, the prospects of finding Poog seemed slim indeed.

"Well, one thing's for sure," said Mr. Beeba, "his purple skin will stand out quite vividly against all this snow. Something of a chiaroscuro effect, if you will."

Spuckler snorted, as if he were having an allergic reaction to Mr. Beeba's vocabulary.

I took a good long look at the valley. It rose to our left and descended sharply to our right. "Which way should we go?"

"Left," Spuckler said. "Folks always build shelter on high ground, so as they can defend themselves 'gainst predators. Poog would do the same, you can betcher boots on that."

"Ah, but Spuckler," Mr. Beeba said, "we must make our decision based not upon whims and fancies, but upon logic and reason. Gax, from which direction is the wind blowing?"

Gax raised his head up on his spindly neck and, with a few mechanical clacks and clicks, extended an antenna into the air.

"FROM THE LEFT."

"Ah! You see?" Mr. Beeba made a grand gesture with his arms. "Clearly we must follow the valley to the right if we are to have the wind at our backs."

There was a pause. I started to say something but stopped.

There was another pause.

"The wind at our *backs*?" Spuckler threw his hands in the air. "You're sayin' we should make decisions based on which way the dadburned *wind* is blowin'?"

Mr. Beeba turned to me. "Akiko, surely you'd agree that having the wind howling in one's face whilst on a strenuous uphill hike is a drearily unpleasant affair, to say nothing of what it does to one's complexion."

"Um, Mr. Beeba . . ."

We were interrupted by a high-pitched warbling sound from above.

Poog!

I craned my neck, trying to find him among the icy cliffs that towered above us. My jaw dropped.

I was looking at not one Poog, but *dozens* of Poogs!

"Heavens," Mr. Beeba said. *"T-Toogolians."*

Chapter 5

There, about thirty yards above us, was a big group of spherical creatures with pale purple skin and glassy black eyes. No arms, legs, or anything else. Just like Poog, except . . .

. . . different.

Some of them had eyes that were smaller than Poog's. Others were bigger than Poog, and still others were more perfectly round. The Toogolians floated down until they surrounded us on all sides, then stopped and just hovered there. They weren't smiling. Far from it. They looked angry.

"Well, I'll be ding-dang-diddled," Spuckler whispered. Obviously I wasn't the only one who had never seen other members of Poog's species before.

The Toogolians said nothing, allowing the silence to stretch on and on. Two of them floated forward. They were apparently the leaders of the group, and they looked *very* angry.

I put one hand on Mr. Beeba's shoulder. "Um, maybe you should say something, Mr. B. You know, apologize for us, uh, breaking all their sacred rules and stuff."

"An excellent suggestion, Akiko." He coughed. Cleared his throat. Coughed again.

"In Toogolian, you mean?" He looked very nervous.

"Of *course* in Toogolian. They wouldn't understand if you spoke in English, would they?"

"Oh, but they would, Akiko," he said. "They are capable of understanding any number of languages, but their vocal cords limit them to *speaking* only in Toogolian."

I thought this over.

"Okay, but I still think you ought to use their native language. They'll have a better impression of us that way."

"Yes. Quite. Yes."

He coughed again.

Our Poog-like visitors looked increasingly hostile.

Spuckler turned to Mr. Beeba. "Come on, Beebs. *Say* something, for cryin' out loud! You're always blabbin' on and on about everything till we wanna stick a rock in your mouth and tape it shut. For once we wantcha to talk—we *want*cha to talk—an' now we can't get a peep outta ya!"

Mr. Beeba's eyes were darting around like crazy. I felt a big confession coming on.

"Look, the fact of the matter is . . ." He looked at the ground. He looked at his hands. ". . . I've always been better at listening comprehension than, er, conversational Toogolian."

That's when it hit me. In all the time I'd known Mr. Beeba, I'd never once heard him actually say a word in Poog's language. I knew from personal experience that it was not an easy language to pronounce. No wonder Mr. Beeba was so nervous.

"Look," I whispered, "it doesn't have to be anything fancy. Just, uh, 'We come in peace,' or 'Please don't kill us.' You know, something like that."

Mr. Beeba frantically scratched his forehead. "Peace . . . peace . . . I *used* to know that word in Toogolian. . . . It was on the final exam . . . just after the multiple-choice questions. . . ."

A loud, warbly gurgling noise erupted from the two Toogolian leaders. Our hosts—captors, I might as well call them—had clearly run out of patience.

"They want to know why we're here," said Mr. Beeba. "They're asking who we work for."

The two Poog look-alikes bobbed up and down in the air, angrily awaiting an answer.

"Beeba," whispered Spuckler, "it's now or never, buddy. You can do it. I *know* ya can." It was just about the gentlest thing I'd ever heard Spuckler say to anyone.

Mr. Beeba cleared his throat, opened his mouth, closed it, opened it again, closed it again, licked his lips, and opened it again.

He said . . .

. . . something.

Toogolian is a very hard language to describe. It's gurgly. It's warbly. It's wiggly and bubbly. It slips, slides, bounces, and burps. It's nearly impossible to write it out in letters of the alphabet.

It's fun to *try*, though.

Mr. Beeba said something like this:

"Oodily-abbily-eedle-a-dabbily-oodle."

Only he said it about five times fast, and once or twice backward. It was very loud and high-pitched.

After he finished, Mr. Beeba had to cough several times. I think he'd hurt his throat.

The Toogolian leaders narrowed their eyes. I'd have expected them to be impressed, but they only looked suspicious. They turned to each other and had a brief gurgly conversation. I noticed that they talked more quickly than they had a moment before, and *much* more quickly than Poog ever had with us. It made me think that Poog was always forcing himself to speak slowly, so that Mr. Beeba would be able to understand and translate for the rest of us.

As the rapid-fire conversation continued, Mr. Beeba tried to explain what he had said to them.

"I apologized for our desecration of the most holy soil of Toog, and promised that we'd break no further laws."

So far, so good.

"At least I *think* I used the right word for laws." He frowned. "I might possibly have said the word for enchiladas."

"Wait a minute," I said. "They have enchiladas on the planet Toog?"

"Not necessarily. They simply have a word that *means* enchiladas."

"Yeah, but why would they invent a word that means enchiladas if they didn't *have* enchiladas to begin with?"

Mr. Beeba looked at me blankly. "I can't answer that question, Akiko. But I can tell you this: The Toogolian word for enchiladas is *devilishly* close to the one for laws."

The Toogolian leaders finished their conversation. They turned to us. One of them, the smaller one, said something short and warbly.

"They still want to know who we work for," said Mr. Beeba.

"Tell 'em we don't work for nobody!" said Spuckler. "We're freelancers."

"No," I said. "Tell them we work for Poog."

Mr. Beeba's eyes popped a bit in surprise, then settled into an expression of understanding. "Yes. We work for Poog. Perfect."

He turned to the Toogolians, cleared his throat again, and spoke in their language, this time much more confidently.

They reacted with skepticism, but after another warbly chat they seemed to accept Mr. Beeba's statement as the truth. For the time being, anyway.

One or two more sentences were exchanged. It was decided that we would follow them to a nearby city, where our fate would be determined by a group of Toogolian elders. The last thing they said to us was the scariest. Mr. Beeba translated it like this:

"Don't try any funny business or we'll brainmelt you."

"*Brainmelt* us?"

"Poog told me about it once," Mr. Beeba said.

"Toogolians possess the ability to turn brains to the consistency of thin porridge. They're not terribly proud of it, mind you. But they hold it in reserve as a means of self-defense. Indeed, it is the threat of brainmelting that has kept Toog free of intruders for so many years."

I shivered a bit. "Man. Here I was thinking Toog would be filled with happy purple Poogs floating around smiling at one another. Turns out they're a bunch of scary little brainmelters."

"Well," Mr. Beeba said, looking as if he wanted to say I was wrong but couldn't, "they're not all cute and cuddly, no."

Chapter 6

We left the ship where it was and began our march. The troop of Toogolians took positions on either side of us like bodyguards. (Or prison guards, depending how you looked at it.) They led us down the valley, to the right, as it turned out.

"What did I tell you?" Mr. Beeba said. "They don't like the wind in their faces any more than I do." Spuckler rolled his eyes at me and—for once—let the comment go unanswered.

As we marched, the icy walls gave way to black stony cliffs and the snowy path changed into a gravelly stream, forcing the Toogolians to guide us to drier ground off to one side. Clearly there was more to Toog than snow and ice: It was starting to feel downright tropical.

After about an hour's hike we came to a place where the valley opened up into a vast plain surrounded by mountains. The area was almost entirely hidden beneath clouds of mist, which rolled lazily from one mountainside to another, never allowing more than a small patch of ground to become visible at any one time. In the center of the plain stood about a dozen jagged outcroppings of stone, tall black towers rising from the mist like cliffs in a Chinese painting. It was a breathtaking scene, but also just a little spooky.

"Shring-la Rai," said Mr. Beeba. "I never thought I'd see it with my own eyes."

"Shingle-Roy?" I asked.

"No, Akiko: Shring-la *Rai*. It is the planet Toog's capital city. Poog has spoken of it many times, always with great reverence."

"City?" asked Spuckler. "I don't see no city. Just a bunch of rocks."

"Look carefully, Spuckler. Toogolian architecture is designed to blend into its surroundings. The tops of those peaks—the upper two-thirds, I'll bet—are not peaks at all, but buildings. *Toogolian* buildings."

"Hmf," grunted Spuckler. "These guys're even weirder than I thought."

Our escorts led us onward, down into the clouds of mist covering the plain. Every once in a while I'd see other gray Poog-like shapes—or even a small procession of them—somewhere deep in the whiteness, floating silently from one place to another.

We came to the base of one of the stone towers. Spuckler rubbed his jaw. "Don't like the looks of this place. Don't much care for this prisoner-of-war treatment we're gettin', neither."

"Don't worry, Spuckler," I said. "Once they see that we're Poog's friends, they'll really roll out the red carpet. Or purple carpet. Or whatever carpet they have."

The Toogolians led us to a large, craggy hole in the wall of the tower—you couldn't really call it a doorway—and we followed them inside. There, in the middle of a circular room, was a large stone with a shiny metal plaque attached to it. Carved on the plaque were strange twisting lines and loops that must have been words in the Toogolian language. Above the stone, hovering in midair, was a small spherical sculpture. It slowly spun around and around, revealing a Poog-like face: concave circles to indicate the eyes, a simple chiseled line for the mouth.

"Zeem," Mr. Beeba said to me, quickly reading the plaque. "Poog's great-uncle. He is one of Toog's greatest statesmen." He raised a finger. "Or *was*, I should say."

"He's dead?"

Mr. Beeba nodded, and indicated that we should keep moving. The Toogolians were leading us past the sculpture and up a steep flight of stairs.

"How did he die?"

"A real tragedy, Akiko. He had gone to negotiate with the Tri-Yarms, a race that once shared this planet with the Toogolians. They ambushed poor Zeem and killed him."

"Whoa. Did the Toogolians go on a big brain-melting rampage?"

"Poog doesn't like to talk about it, so I can't tell you much about what happened during those troubled times. But this I *do* know: All the Tri-Yarms were forced to leave the planet Toog, and today not a single one of them is to be found here."

The stony staircase curved around and around. Soon we had climbed high above the misty floor of the valley, and Mr. Beeba and I were starting to huff and puff like a couple of old men. Even Spuckler was looking a bit winded.

Finally we arrived at a round wooden door. Mr. Beeba swallowed noisily. "This is it. They're taking us in to see the elders."

Spuckler grunted and folded his arms. "Elders. Just what I need: a bunch of wrinkly old Poogs givin' me the evil eye."

"Hush, Spuckler," Mr. Beeba said. "This is *not* an occasion for your usual impudent swagger. We must treat our hosts with the utmost respect."

I touched Spuckler on the arm. "He's right, Spuckler. Try to go easy on the sassy comments, all right? I don't want any of us going home with a melted brain."

Gax rattled a bit, as if to show his agreement.

The smaller of the two Toogolian leaders faced the door and said something loud and very musical, like a Gregorian chant being played at double speed.

There was a pause: total silence.

Then the door opened.

Beyond it was another wide circular room. In the very center of this room, sunken in the floor, was a huge, rough piece of stone, black and craggy, speckled with moss.

On the other side of the room floated nine Poog creatures, spread out in a single row, all hovering about three feet above the floor. The one in the center looked to be the oldest: He was shriveled up like an old apple, with dark spots covering his pale purple skin. The next two on either side of him were less wrinkled, and the next two, and the next two until . . .

Poog!

There he was on the far left side, floating in silence. I wanted to run over and give him a big hug, but something stopped me. Maybe it was the frown he was wearing. Who am I kidding? *Definitely* it was the frown he was wearing. He didn't seem the least bit pleased to see us.

I shot a glance at Mr. Beeba and Spuckler. They looked equally troubled. Was Poog angry with us? I mean, he *had* told us not to follow him, but come on, we were his best friends. How could we *not* follow him?

He sure *looked* angry, though.

The two Toogolian guards bowed, as did the troop of Toogolians behind us. Mr. Beeba bowed deeply and indicated with a panicky grimace that we were to do the same.

One of the Toogolian elders—a small, lumpy-
looking guy on the far right side—spoke first. I'll bet it
was something along the lines of "State your business."

The smaller of the two guards said something warbly

and gurgly. He sounded very nervous, like a student reporting before the school principal.

Mr. Beeba whispered a quick translation:

"We found these four intruders . . . in the snows above Shring-la Rai. . . . They appear to be unarmed. . . . One of them speaks a queer approximation of our language. . . ."

(Mr. Beeba grew red in the face as he translated that last bit.)

"They claim . . . forgive me if I offend by repeating lies . . . they claim to be friends of Elder Poog."

The eight Toogolian elders to the right of Poog turned and stared at him suspiciously.

Poog avoided our eyes and gave a stuttering, gurgly answer.

Mr. Beeba gasped.

He shook his head before translating.

"He says . . . Poog says . . ."

He swallowed and shook his head again.

"What?" Spuckler said. "Come on, spit it out!"

"He says he's never seen us before in his life."

chapter 7

I couldn't believe it. I wouldn't *let* myself believe it. Why would Poog say such a thing? It was bad enough that he wasn't happy to see us, but to claim he didn't even *know* us? Here we were, going through so much trouble because we wanted to help him, and now *this!*

One of the shriveled Toogolian elders spoke briefly and decisively.

Mr. Beeba's eyes opened wide. "They're going to have us imprisoned until further notice."

The two guards bowed and led us back out of the room. I tried to catch Poog's attention, but he wouldn't let his eyes meet mine. The last I saw of him was a frown and a glassy stare aimed at nothing in particular.

Then we were out of the room and stumbling back down to the bottom of the tower. I had this weird dizzy feeling and a pain in my stomach. Part of me wished I were back in Middleton.

"Incomprehensible!" Mr. Beeba was angry, but was holding himself down to a whisper. "How could he *do* this to us?"

"PERHAPS HE'S BEEN BRAINWASHED," Gax said. "NONMECHANICAL BRAINS ARE OFTEN SUBJECT TO STRESS-RELATED DELUSIONS." He paused, than added, "NO DISRESPECT INTENDED TO NONMECHANICAL BRAINS IN *GENERAL*, OF COURSE."

Spuckler was furious, and not quite speaking in complete sentences. "Well, of all the dagnabbed . . . Riskin' life an' limb . . . Why, I oughta . . . We're only tryin' to give the feller a *hand*!" He snorted like a bull in a ring. "That little purple puck-head's got a lot t' answer for, I'll tell ya that much!"

"Now, hang on," I said. "There's got to be some good reason for this. Maybe . . . maybe that wasn't the real Poog."

"Ah yes," Mr. Beeba said, "the old evil twin idea. That would explain a great number of things. Perhaps he's got the *real* Poog locked up in a dungeon some-where. Or was *that* the real Poog, having been brain-washed *by* the evil twin?"

"There ain't no evil twin!" Spuckler barked. "That was Poog, pure an' simple. He's turned on us, an' that's that!"

I didn't want to admit it, but Spuckler's explanation seemed the most likely. For whatever reason, Poog no longer wanted to be associated with us. The question now was would he ever acknowledge us as his friends again? My stomach was really starting to hurt.

We exited the tower and plunged back into the fog. Our Toogolian captors led us quickly through the mist, past shadowy buildings and distant flickering flames, until we came to a tall wooden post at the edge of the city, rising from the ground like a totem pole.

One of the guards said something, which Mr. Beeba translated as, simply, "Climb."

There were just enough toeholds in the post for us to scale it. I went first, followed by Mr. Beeba, with Spuckler and Gax bringing up the rear. The Toogolians floated along beside us, looking as if they were just waiting for an excuse to turn our brains to mush. If being locked up meant getting away from the guards, I was beginning to look forward to it.

After climbing at least two or three hundred feet, we reached the top of the post. A platform about ten feet square had been built there out of rough wooden planks. We crawled through a door, which the Toogolians—using some sort of telekinetic power—caused to lock behind us. Then they sank out of sight, presumably to stand guard at the bottom of the post.

We were in an open-air prison: a ten-by-ten-foot platform that we couldn't leave, save by leaping off and falling hundreds of feet to the ground.

The sky had gone from dirty white to charcoal gray: Night was coming. With no blankets it was hard to stay warm, but Spuckler got Gax's torch going, and that provided a bit of heat.

I rubbed my hands in front of Gax's flame. "Maybe they'll just, uh, deport us or something."

"Not likely," Mr. Beeba said. He'd fallen into a sour mood. "Without Poog speaking in our defense, we can just about consider our brains melted."

"BUT I DON'T HAVE A BRAIN," Gax said. "NOT A *REAL* ONE, ANYWAY."

"Yes, Gax, you lucky devil. Never in my life have I so dearly wished to be brainless."

Spuckler had become strangely upbeat. "Well, it don't do us no good to sit around frettin'. Best we can do is get some shut-eye." He lay down on his back and closed his eyes.

Mr. Beeba and I exchanged a few more words.

"I don't get it," I said. "What happened to this big crisis we came here for? Everything seems to be just fine on the planet Toog."

Mr. Beeba gazed into the darkness. "A crisis is not always big and noisy, Akiko."

"What's that supposed to mean? There's something you haven't told me, isn't there?"

"Only this." His eyes met mine. "There's something valuable on this planet. Or *in* this planet. Under its surface."

"What, like diamonds or something?"

"Possibly. Poog mentioned it to me years ago, but I can't remember what it was. Something . . . valuable."

"All right, so there's something valuable here. What's the problem?"

"Where there is something valuable," Mr. Beeba said, "there are always problems, Akiko. Mark my words."

And with that, Mr. Beeba went to sleep.

I soon did the same.

Or tried to, anyway. It took me a long time. I stared up into the cloudy blackness, trying not to think of the one thing that was really getting to me, the thing that troubled me more than the weird invisible crisis, more than the possibility of having my brain melted. The thing that really bothered me came down to a single question.

Was this the end of my friendship with Poog?

Chapter 8

At first I thought it was a dream.

doo-kaaak . . .

doo-kaaak . . .

doo-kaaak . . .

But eventually the noise became loud enough to wake me up.

DOO-KAAAK . . .

DOO-KAAAK . . .

DOO-KAAAK . . .

A mechanical sound. Like something from a factory.

I rubbed my eyes, sat up, and looked around. The cloudy sky was still a dull dark gray. Spuckler and Mr. Beeba were dead asleep; they sounded like two guys having a snoring contest. Gax, alert as always, had his head turned toward the source of the *doo-kaaak doo-kaaak.*

"What is it, Gax?"

"I'M NOT SURE, MA'AM. IT MUST BE *VERY* BIG, THOUGH."

"Can you see any of it?"

"NO, MA'AM. IT'S HIDDEN BY THE MOUNTAIN RANGE. THE ONLY THING I HAVE TO GO ON IS THE SOUND."

DOO-KAAAK . . .

DOO-KAAAK . . .

DOO-KAAAK . . .

I cupped my hands around my ears to catch as much of it as possible. "Weird. It doesn't sound very . . . *Toogolian,* does it?"

"NO, MA'AM, IT DOESN'T."

We sat there listening to the noise for five or six minutes. The planet Toog was so quiet, so peaceful. This new sound was disturbingly out of place.

"YOU MIGHT AS WELL TRY TO GET SOME SLEEP, MA'AM." Gax's torch flickered a bit, casting jittery shadows. "I'LL WAKE YOU IF THERE ARE ANY DEVELOPMENTS."

I didn't want to sleep. But I *was* tired.

I lay down and closed my eyes. The noise, though troubling, was almost hypnotic. It repeated so regularly, so endlessly. . . .

doo-kaaak . . .

   doo-kaaak . . .

      doo-kaaak . . .

Within minutes I was asleep again.

But not for long.

"WAKE UP, MA'AM."

Gax. Talking to me.

"WAKE UP, MA'AM. SOMETHING'S COMING."

I'd fallen into a much deeper sleep this time, and it was a real struggle to tear myself out of it. I forced my eyes to open. The sky looked a little lighter than before, but daybreak was still a long way off.

"SOMETHING'S COMING TOWARD US. A LARGE IN-ANIMATE OBJECT."

"A what?"

"AN OBJECT. FROM BENEATH THE PLATFORM."

I was up now, but still groggy. Gax had his neck stretched out as far as it would go, allowing his eyes to peer over the edge of the wooden planks.

"Beneath the platform?"

"IT'S ALMOST HERE."

"What? *What's* almost here?"

"HERE IT IS."

I swallowed hard as a shadowy square-ish shape rose over the edge of the wooden boards. It was at least ten feet wide and maybe fifteen feet long. I blinked. There before my eyes, just barely legible in the darkness, were the words . . .

. . . MIDDLETON POLICE.

It was the spaceship car! But . . . but *how?*

A light went on inside. There in the front seat, floating behind the wheel, was Poog.

"Poog!" I was so happy to see him—so relieved—it was impossible to be angry about how he'd acted earlier.

He smiled. He blurted out something in Toogolian. It sounded very gentle, but somehow also very urgent. I turned to Gax.

"You don't, uh . . ."

"I'M AFRAID NOT, MA'AM. NOT A WORD."

Poog repeated whatever he'd said, even more urgently.

"We'd better wake the others."

It took some doing—some pinching and jostling, to be exact—but eventually we managed to get both Spuckler and Mr. Beeba to open their eyes. Spuckler was delighted to see the spaceship, but much *less* delighted to see Poog. Mr. Beeba, like me, must have sensed that Poog had returned to normal. We felt like a *team* again.

For the third time Poog tried to get his message across.

"Poog says for us to climb in," Mr. Beeba said. "He's going to help us escape."

Spuckler was unconvinced. "Yeah, right. This is the same guy who said he didn't even *know* us a few hours ago."

Poog looked embarrassed, frustrated. He said something with a pleading expression in his eyes.

"He says he'll explain about that later."

Spuckler twisted his lips like he wanted to spit.

"Come on, Spuckler," I said. "It's not like we have any other choice. None of us is very happy about what Poog did back there . . ."

Poog winced.

". . . but we've got to trust him. He's our friend. The only friend we've *got* on this planet."

Spuckler still wasn't buying it. But I don't think he wanted to stay on that platform any more than I did. We all piled into the space car and got ready to go. Spuckler took the driver's seat and shifted into gear. The engine rumbled a bit, but the ship didn't budge.

"Hmm," said Spuckler. "Engine trouble," he added,

though it sounded more like a question than a statement. He yanked several levers up and down, but the ship stayed exactly where it was.

Gax was the first to locate the source of the problem. "IT'S THE PLATFORM, SIR," he said.

"The platform?" said Spuckler.

"IT'S *GOT* US!"

Chapter 9

Through the rear window I saw that the wooden platform . . . well, there's no other way to put it: It was alive! What looked to be several tentacle-like growths had emerged from its sides and snapped onto the ship, holding us there like a bug in a Venus's flytrap.

Spuckler groaned. "I *knew* it was too easy!"

"Thramblewood!" Mr. Beeba said. "But of course! I should have recognized the grain of those floorboards."

Another bark-covered tentacle lashed out and flung itself around the ship, this time falling straight across the windshield.

My heart was pounding like crazy. "Wh-what is it doing? Is it going to *eat* us?"

"Impossible, Akiko," Mr. Beeba said. "Thramble-wood is incapable of digesting flesh. It lacks the proper enzymes." But then: "Or does it? I could be thinking of *thrumble*wood; I'm always confusing the two."

Spuckler had crawled out the passenger window and was trying to pry the wooden tentacles away, but with little success. "Dagnabbit! There'll be a whole mess of Poog's buddies up here b'fore ya know it!" I wished he hadn't said that. Now I had two deaths to choose from: flesh-eating thramblewood or brainmelting Toogolians.

That's when I noticed Poog busily muttering something over and over again.

"Some sort of incantation, no doubt," Mr. Beeba said. "He'll get us out of this, just you wait!" From the looks of things, though, Poog was having trouble recalling the magic words.

Gax had joined Spuckler outside the ship and was sawing through the branches with his rotary blade. But with every wrist-thick tentacle he severed, two more sprang out to ensnare us, and there was no way Gax could keep up. On the contrary, he was just barely managing to dodge the branches as they tried to latch on to *him*.

Poog narrowed his eyes and redoubled his efforts to

find the right incantation. By that time the windows were half buried under branches crisscrossing this way and that, and Spuckler was choked in tentacles that had snaked themselves around his legs.

Mr. Beeba was doing his best to keep up morale. "That's right, Poog. . . . You're almost there. . . . Take your time. . . ." He was trying to appear calm and failing miserably.

THRAP!

One branch as wide as my waist encircled the ship and began to tighten. There was a sickening groan as the frame of the cabin started to give way.

"I thought you said it wasn't going to eat us!" I shouted at Mr. Beeba.

"It *isn't* eating us," he cried. "It's *crushing* us!"

"SIR . . . I . . . I . . ."

Through the web of branches I could just make out the shape of Gax. Six or seven tentacles had finally got hold of him and were writhing around his body like boa constrictors. They had wrestled Gax's blade to a spot in the air where it whizzed and whirred but touched nothing.

"I . . . I . . . I . . ."

"Don't worry, li'l buddy!" Spuckler cried. "I'll save ya!" But Spuckler was in no position to save anyone, himself included. By this time he was so deeply caught in the branches, we could hardly even see him.

Finally Poog blurted out something . . .

ZUTT-ZUTT-ZUTT

. . . and the branches came to a full stop.

There was a moment of quiet, during which none of us dared even breathe a sigh of relief.

The silence continued.

Poog closed his eyes.

Breathed in, breathed out.

He repeated what he'd just said, giving it a *very* slightly different intonation.

The branches shuddered a bit, then began constricting again, faster than before.

GRUH-GRUNK!

The roof of the car nearly caved in.

PAAAASH!

One of the windows shattered.

Mr. Beeba snapped. He grabbed Poog and held him between his palms.

"Say it *right*, you fool!"

Poog stared at Mr. Beeba in shock.

66

Mr. Beeba swallowed so hard it sounded like he was choking. He let go of Poog and turned his hands into a knot of fingers. "Er, I mean . . . in view of our present circumstances . . . it *behooves* us to, erm . . . strive for *accuracy*. . . ."

Poog ignored him and took one more shot at saying the magic words.

FLAP!

FLEPP!

FLOOP!

The branches sucked themselves back like a dozen tape measures recoiling at once. The platform . . .

FLUPP! FLOP! FLUTT!

. . . went back . . .

ZUPP! ZOOT! ZIPPLE!

. . . to being a platform.

We were all free and clear.

Spuckler made a terrific whooping noise and threw the ship into the highest of its high gears. There was a rumble, a grumble, a deafening boom.

A moment later the pole, the platform, and all of Shring-la Rai were miles and miles away. We zoomed out into the cloudy night sky of Toog, and off to . . .

. . . wherever it was that we were going.

Chapter 10

As we rocketed over the mountains, Poog turned to me with an expression of great nervousness. He hesitated, sighed. It seemed hard for him to look me straight in the eye.

Finally he opened his mouth. He spoke quietly, slowly, pausing every so often to allow for Mr. Beeba's translations.

"Poog says, first of all, that he wants to apologize. He knows it must have come as a great shock to have him deny us in public."

"You can say *that* again."

"Hush, Akiko. Don't rub it in."

Poog continued.

"The fact of the matter is," Mr. Beeba said, sounding just as surprised to be saying it as I was to be hearing it, "Poog is not *supposed* to know us."

At this point Poog began to speak more quickly. It was as if he'd thrown open a latch on a long-locked cupboard, allowing its contents to come tumbling out. Mr. Beeba translated breathlessly.

"Poog left his home planet many years ago to embark on a century-long period of meditation, a time of absolute quiet and solitude. He was to wander the very edges of the universe, lost in his thoughts, unencumbered by the material world. He was supposed to be alone. Completely alone."

"But why?"

"I'm not entirely sure why. It's something all the

Toogolian elders are expected to do, part of their training. Sounds deathly dull, doesn't it?"

Poog sighed again, then continued.

"During the thirty-sixth year of his meditations, he found that he could take the isolation no longer. He ceased his wanderings and headed straight for the nearest populated planet."

"Smoo!"

"Really, Akiko, you're absolutely *ruining* the dramatic effect of my translation," said Mr. Beeba. "But yes, it was Smoo, that's right."

Poog seemed to relax. He'd made what was for him a terrible confession, and now he was past the worst of it.

"He knew that he shouldn't stay long, that he should return to his meditations as quickly as possible. And yet as he made friends on the planet Smoo—"

"Me an' Gax, ya mean," Spuckler said.

Mr. Beeba squinted angrily.

"*Ahem.* As he made friends on the planet Smoo, he found that he grew more and more attached to the place. After several years, he realized his meditations were over, and that he would never renew them."

Poog's eyes, which had been glazed over with memories of the past, seemed to focus a bit more. His expression toughened.

"When news came to him of the crisis on Toog, he knew he would at last be confronted by the other elders, that he'd have to tell them about his abandoned training. But when the time came to do so, he lost his nerve. He said nothing, and allowed them to believe his solitude had continued unbroken to this day."

"Wow," I said. "Poog lied."

"No, no, Akiko. He simply neglected to tell the complete truth. There's a difference."

"Really?"

Mr. Beeba hesitated and scratched his head. "There's a *bit* of a difference. Surely."

Poog looked at me expectantly. He was finished, and all that remained was my reaction.

"Well, Poog," I said, "I understand. Sort of. You're a Toogolian elder, and that's a big honor, and part of being a Toogolian elder is . . . is not being friends with us."

Poog nodded sadly.

"So maybe the best thing we could do for you right now is just to . . . go away and stop . . . making things difficult for you."

I immediately wished I hadn't said it. It sounded so awful.

He replied quickly, without the slightest hesitation.

"Poog says no," said Mr. Beeba. "He wants us to stay. *Needs* us to stay. He'll deal with the elders later if he has to."

I smiled at Poog. He tried to smile back, but there was a sadness he couldn't quite conceal.

Spuckler turned around in the front seat to join the conversation. "Well, I don't blame ya for givin' up on yer medications, Poog."

"Medi*ta*tions!" said Mr. Beeba.

"Sounds like a big ol' waste of time to me. An' jus' think of all the fun you'd have missed out on if ya hadn't met me."

Mr. Beeba rolled his eyes. Poog and I grinned.

"So Poog," I said, "maybe you'd better tell us what the big problem is here on Toog. If there's a crisis going on, we sure haven't seen any of it yet."

Mr. Beeba leaned forward to get a better view through the windshield.

"I think the answer to your question is standing right there in front of us."

Chapter 11

There in the distance, surrounded by snow-capped mountain ranges, stood a big . . .

. . . a *really* big . . .

. . . thing.

What should I call it? A city with legs? A portable factory? It was larger than gigantic, bigger than humongous. It was at least two miles from one side to the other: a vast saucer-shaped structure with towers and turrets rising from its upper surface and spindly robotic arms jutting out from its sides. It was supported by ten massive columns that bent in several places, like the legs of a mammoth mechanical insect. Every last inch of it was covered in sheets of steely armor.

"Man oh mannfred manganese!" Spuckler cried. "An F-48 core eater!"

"ONE OF THE EARLY MODELS," said Gax. "BEFORE THEY WERE OUTLAWED."

All at once the gigantic mechanized beast began to move. Its legs carried it lumberingly from where it had first stood to a spot a hundred yards or so to the right. Every step made the surrounding mountains shake and echo with the noise. When it came to a stop, a robotic arm descended and began probing the surface of the planet, making a sound that was already familiar to me, though it took a second or two for me to recognize it:

DOO-KAAAK . . .

DOO-KAAAK . . .

DOO-KAAAK . . .

"What in heaven's name is it?" Mr. Beeba said. "I'm afraid *this* sort of hardware is quite beyond my field of reference."

"A core eater's a kinda oil rig an' refinery all in one," Spuckler explained, "an' this core eater is the gran'-mama of 'em all. If needs be, it can drill a hole clear through the planet. They must be after some sort of fuel here on Toog. That would explain that big ol' transport cruiser we saw when we first got here. Once they find what they're after, they'll start processin' it an' transferrin' it up an' off the planet."

Poog narrowed his eyes and said something in unusually slow Toogolian. It sounded like he was announcing a death sentence.

"Never!" Mr. Beeba said. "So *that's* what keeps Toog from freezing over."

"What?" I asked. "What does?"

"Glagma."

"*Glagma?*"

FOOOOOOOOOM!

A white-hot ball of fire shot by us, missing the ship by a matter of one or two feet.

FOOOOOM! SHOOOOM! FLOOOOM!

Another. And another. Then two more.

"Drobe mines!" cried Spuckler. "Hunnerds of 'em!"

STRRRROOOOOM!

One of them glanced off the roof, just barely; still, it was enough to rattle us all like an earthquake.

"Gotta vamoose!" Spuckler hammered buttons and yanked levers all over the dashboard. "Time's a-wastin'!"

FLOOOM! STROOOOM!

Two more near misses.

"Get us out of here, you nincompoop!" Mr. Beeba cried. "Now! Nownownownownow . . ."

FLAAAAAAAAAAAAAAAAAAMM!

A direct hit. Debris everywhere. Smoke so thick it burned my eyes.

Drobe mines whizzed by on all sides. Spuckler grabbed the steering wheel in one hand and hammered buttons with the other. Finally he got the ship turned in the right direction and . . .

BRRRUUUUMMMM!

. . . off we went! Spuckler sent us corkscrewing through the air, zooming off over the mountains at top speed.

SSSSSSSSSHHHH

As I tumbled from one side of the backseat to the other, I caught a glimpse outside through the rear window: Three drobe mines were still on our tail.

"Dagnab the dungle-dorfer!" Spuckler drove the ship through a series of narrow gorges. Black surfaces raced by as we zoomed under bridges of ice and careened over sheer cliffs. At one point he sent us barreling right in toward a snowbank before veering off to one side.

PLLUUUUMMM!

A muffled explosion echoed from behind us.

"That's one of 'em!" cried Spuckler.

I peered out the window: Sure enough, only two drobe mines remained. They were gaining on us, though.

Gax shuddered, and Mr. Beeba wheezed as if he were being strangled.

Spuckler changed direction yet again. This time we started climbing up through the air . . .

. . . up, up, up . . .

. . . higher, higher . . .

. . . the drobe mines in hot pursuit . . .

. . . then:

"Hold on to yer big bony behinds!"

Spuckler steered the ship into a nosedive.

"No!" Mr. Beeba cried.

"Oh yeah!" said Spuckler.

We were now plummeting, flying directly toward a huge slab of snow-speckled stone below.

I should have shut my eyes, but I didn't. For some reason, when you're about to die, you want to see how it happens.

The hard black surface of the stone rushed up to greet us. The drobe mines were still right behind us.

Mr. Beeba said something like, "Fslewy," before fainting again.

Down we went, faster, faster. . . .

Impact was seconds away.

Then . . .

. . . suddenly . . .

. . . *impossibly* . . .

. . . Spuckler made the ship come out of its nosedive and level off.

KRUTT-KRUTT-KRUTT-KRUTT

We grazed the surface of the stone, sending sparks flying. I tried to keep my head high enough to see what was happening behind us, but . . .

PLOOOOMMM! FFLOOOOM!

. . . all I saw were flares of orange-yellow light bathing nearby cliffs as somewhere beyond my field of vision the two drobe mines struck the ground and exploded.

Spuckler howled with delight as we tore off over the mountains and up into the clouds.

I collapsed into the backseat and waited for my heart to stop thudding.

"Somebody promise me," I said to anyone who was still conscious, "that we're not going to see any more drobe mines from now on."

"That's the last of 'em, yeah," said Spuckler. "For sure."

I closed my eyes and let my head roll loose on my shoulders.

Spuckler whistled a little tune, then added:

"Last of 'em for a *while*, anyway."

Chapter 12

Spuckler took the ship higher and higher into the clouds until we began to pass through the upper reaches of Toog's atmosphere. I stared out the windows at the clouds. Mr. Beeba awoke with a start, and—though he grumbled a bit at first—apparently decided to skip his usual criticisms of Spuckler and go right to the heart of our current dilemma.

"If that core eater succeeds in drilling to the center of Toog, the entire planet is doomed," he said. "And though I admit the word *doomed* is one I employ rather too frequently," he added, "in these circumstances I'm afraid it is the only term that applies."

"I don't get it," I said. "How can a single core eater ruin the whole planet?"

Mr. Beeba squinted a bit and drew in his breath. If there had been a blackboard behind him, he'd have grabbed a piece of chalk and begun pacing back and forth in front of it.

"Akiko, you must first keep in mind that Toog is much, much farther from its sun than, say, your home planet of Earth. As a result, it should by all rights be a frozen wasteland, an expanse of ice so bitterly cold as to preclude even the hardiest bacterium from surviving here."

He made his fingers dance, as if trying to conjure up an image of microorganisms freezing to death by the millions.

"And yet the surface of Toog is in many places— Shring-la Rai, for example—quite warm and perfectly hospitable." He paused for effect. "How can that be?"

I thought about this for a moment. Slowly the pieces of the puzzle began to slide together in my head.

"It's heated . . . ," I said, ". . . from *inside*?"

"Precisely!" Mr. Beeba snapped his fingers, and Gax made a few congratulatory popping noises. "At the core of Toog is a substance called glagma, a heat-producing material that is one of the universe's most perfect sources of energy. A single thimbleful can fuel an entire squadron of space cruisers for months at a time. Years, even. It is as valuable throughout the universe as gold is on your home planet."

Spuckler turned around from the front seat. "So that there core eater is trying to suck all the glagma out of the middle of Toog, eh? Gotta hand it to 'em, they know buried treasure when they see it."

"Indeed. Once they find a clear path to the core," Mr. Beeba explained, "they'll draw out every last drop of the glagma, pump it up to that transport cruiser, and leave Toog as a frozen, uninhabitable ball of ice. The Toogolians will have to choose between abandoning the planet they hold so dear, and staying behind to join it in a slow, frozen death."

Total silence. From what I knew about the Toogolians, it seemed clear that the second option was the only one they'd consider.

"Just one question," I said, though I had many, many more. "Who is 'they'? Who's controlling that core eater?"

Poog spoke at length. He was more animated now. Less frightened or sad, more desperate to take action, any action.

"Poog says the identity of the invaders is the central

mystery of this whole crisis," Mr. Beeba said. "Normally Toogolians have a sort of sixth sense about these things, but there's something emanating from that core eater—a psychic static—that prevents them from discerning any specific information about who is behind all this."

"Has anyone tried sneaking inside?"

"The drobe mines present a formidable obstacle. No Toogolian dares go anywhere near that core eater. Meanwhile, the elders talk and squabble about what to do, but never settle upon a real plan of action. They seem already to have given up hope."

I watched Poog as he spoke. I could see that he was not going to give up. Not now, not ever.

"SIR, WHERE EXACTLY ARE YOU TAKING US?" We were now out among the stars, and Toog was growing smaller and smaller behind us. "I DON'T SEE HOW WE'RE GOING TO SOLVE TOOG'S PROBLEMS BY LEAVING THE PLANET."

"We need somebody who knows more about core eaters than I do," Spuckler said. "Somebody who knows all there *is* to know about drobe mines. And I know just who that somebody is."

I leaned forward. Something about Spuckler's upbeat tone was contagious. "You *do*?"

"Course I do."

He turned and said nothing, clearly enjoying the attention.

"Well, come on," said Mr. Beeba. "Who is it?"

"Fella by the name of Ragstubble."

"Ragstubble?"

"That's right. Ragstubble. Fluggly Ragstubble."

The way he said it, you'd have thought he was talking about Superman and Albert Einstein rolled into one. Somehow the name alone made me think the solution to Toog's troubles might be at hand.

"Fluggly Ragstubble," I said. "Can't wait to meet him."

We sailed past the stars for an hour or two before arriving at a nearby planet larger than Toog and—judging from its sandy orange surface—a good deal warmer.

"I ain't seen Fluggly in years," Spuckler said as we plunged into the planet's atmosphere. "We were pals back in school."

Mr. Beeba gasped. *"You* went to *school*? Impossible."

"Sure I did. An' I gra-jee-ated with honors, too."

"No way," I said, then quickly added, "I mean, wow, that's great."

Mr. Beeba narrowed his eyes. "What *sort* of school?"

"The Acme-Andromeda Academy of Carburetor Maintenance and Repair."

"Ah," said Mr. Beeba. "I thought you meant a *real* school."

"They don't get no realer," Spuckler said. "Now, Fluggly, he was the smartest guy in the whole class. He once broke apart a Frazzner-Gockling D-78 Thrumple engine and put it back together in twenty-three seconds. Blindfolded *and* with his nose plugged."

(I'm not exactly sure how the nose plugging made the feat more impressive, but apparently it did.)

By now we were shooting across the surface of the planet, past great orange hills and over cactus-covered plains. Spuckler killed the engine as we approached a big fenced-in compound. It was about the size of a school-yard, littered with huge rusting engines and half-assembled rocket ships propped up on cinder blocks. The air reeked of diesel fuel and charcoal smoke. A clanking noise echoed from a shack at the center of it all.

"Somebody *lives* here?" I asked.

"Ain't it great?" Spuckler jumped out of the ship and ran over to the gate. "Wait'll ya meet Fluggly," he added as he threw the gate open and strolled right on in. "He's a hoot. Jus' like me."

Mr. Beeba and I shot each other a worried glance. Having one Spuckler on our team was a little risky. But *two* of them? That sounded downright dangerous.

Chapter 13

"**Fluggs!**" cried **Spuckler.** "It's yer ol' pal Spuck! Getcher fuzzy butt out here an' show me how big your belly is!"

The clanking stopped. There was a brief rustling inside the shack, followed by a sudden bang as a door flew open on one side, knocking over several crates of scrap steel.

Out came a big, hairy troll of a man, as tall as Spuckler but much more heavyset. He had one huge eyebrow, two beady little eyes, and one big horn a little too far to one side of his forehead. He was dressed in a raggedy, oil-stained mechanic's suit with pockets and pouches all over the place, and dozens of tools attached at the waist that clinked and clunked with every move he made. The oddest thing about him was that he had three arms: two on his left side and just one on his right. He immediately lunged forward and snatched Spuckler up in a bear hug that would have left me flat as a used tube of toothpaste.

"Spuckler Boach!" he barked. "You no-good bacon-burnin' lyin' cheatin' lizard-stealin' two-bit weasel-eatin' varmint!" If he had smiled any harder, he'd have shattered his teeth.

"Fluggly Ragstubble!" Spuckler howled. "You low-rent worm-chewin' two-timin' snotty-nosed good-for-nothin' scab-pickin' belly-button-lickin' ragamuffin!"

What followed was something like a cross between the Texas two-step and an all-out brawl. They were so happy to see each other, the only way they could get their joy across was by pounding arms, smacking backs, butting heads,

and just generally seeing who could leave who more black, blue, and bruised all over. At first I was scared they'd hurt each other, but soon I was giggling like crazy. I couldn't help myself: They looked like they were having so much fun. Gax rocked happily from side to side, and even Mr. Beeba was grinning.

But Poog . . .

. . . Poog was not happy. He was staring at Fluggly Ragstubble with a look of real . . . I don't know, *disgust*. Like he was looking at a monster-sized cockroach. Poog floated backward, as if he wanted to flee altogether.

And when Ragstubble laid eyes on Poog, the reaction was hardly any better.

"Spuck," he said, one arm frozen in mid-punch, "tell me that's not a Toogolian you got over there." His beady eyes got even beadier.

"Well, sure, Fluggs," Spuckler said. "This here is Poog, from the planet Toog. He's the whole reason we're out here to see ya."

Ragstubble grunted and exhaled slowly.

"I'm Akiko," I said, jumping forward. Whatever his problem was with Poog, I figured distracting him wouldn't hurt. "I'm from the planet Earth. Um, real far away from here. Nice place, though. We've got our own, uh, moon and everything."

Ragstubble reached out and shook my hand gently, his eyes never leaving Poog's.

"This here's Beeba," Spuckler said.

"*Mr.* Beeba," said Mr. Beeba.

"He's kind of a dork," Spuckler whispered a little too loudly, "but a fairly decent guy, once ya get to know him."

Ragstubble shook Mr. Beeba's hand just as he'd shaken mine, his eyes glued to Poog's. Poog, for his part, now wore an equally hostile expression. What was the deal? Did these two already *know* each other?

"And you remember Gax, don'tcha? I had him with me back at the academy."

Ragstubble took his eyes off Poog long enough to wink at Gax. "How you doin', little guy?" he said. He was smiling, but the sound of fun and games had vanished from his voice.

"QUITE WELL, SIR, THANK YOU," Gax replied.

There was an awkward pause. Spuckler, Ragstubble, and I all started to say something, then all stopped at the same time.

Another awkward pause.

"Well now, Spuck," Ragstubble said, his eyes returning to Poog. "What brings you here?"

Spuckler began to explain about Toog, and the core eater, and the drobe mines. When he got to the part about the glagma, Ragstubble interrupted.

"Don't waste your breath, Spuck. I know all about glagma. All about how much of it there is buried down in the core of Toog. All about how the Toogolians don't want to lose a single molecule of the stuff."

"Ya do?"

"Of course I do," Ragstubble said, planting two of his hands on his hips and rubbing his jaw with the third. "My people *come* from Toog."

Chapter 14

Ragstubble invited all of us into his shack. By the expression on his face, I think he wanted Poog to stay outside, but he didn't say so. Then again, Poog didn't look as though he was exactly dying to join the party.

The inside of the shack was a cross between a hardware store and a junkyard. There were engines and tailpipes and buckets full of enormous spark plugs; there were machines that looked like they'd gotten stranded somewhere between being put together and ripped apart. In the middle of it all was a cast-iron stove, its fire blazing inside, with a big black pot on top that—considering the stench it was producing—I sincerely hoped wasn't dinner.

Ragstubble invited us to sit down on various barrels and overturned crates he dragged into a rough circle around the stove. We did as we were told. All of us but Poog, that is. He stayed right where he was near the door, as if he wanted to make sure he'd be the first one out.

"I'm a Tri-Yarm," said Ragstubble, sitting down and sloshing the contents of the pot with a wooden spoon. "Guess you already knew that, Spuck. But what a lot of people don't know is that we Tri-Yarms originally lived on the planet Toog. Years ago, before . . ." He shot a cold glance at Poog. ". . . before the Toogolians drove us out."

Ragstubble reached into the pot and pulled up something slimy, green, and alive. He popped it in his mouth and chewed. Finally he made a face, spat it out, and tossed it back into the pot.

"A little rare."

I was trying to remember what Mr. Beeba had said to me back when we were being taken to see the elders. Something about the Tri-Yarms. Something about them killing Poog's great-uncle. I figured this was as good a time as any to get the facts straight, and it seemed to me that Ragstubble knew the facts pretty well.

"Why did the Toogolians make your people leave? They must have had reasons."

"Reasons," he repeated. He opened a tin and threw some black powder into the pot. "Sure. Toogolians have reasons. They *always* have reasons. They attacked us; we defended ourselves. I guess they didn't like that."

Poog, who had remained angry but silent, could control himself no longer. He opened his mouth and let loose a barrage of warbly syllables, faster and louder than I'd ever heard from him before. And then—this is the really incredible thing—Ragstubble answered him right back in Toogolian, his rough, husky voice blurting the gurgly sounds out confidently, effortlessly. Poog responded, louder than before, and Ragstubble cut him off, jumping to his feet and jabbing a finger in Poog's direction. Poog flew through the air right up to Ragstubble's face, words shooting out of his mouth, his eyes angry, defiant.

"Hey hey hey!" I leaped between the two of them with my arms stretched out. They glared at one another as if I weren't even there. But they became quiet.

"You two need to cool off." Ragstubble made a little snorting noise, sat down, and turned his attention back

to the bubbling pot. Poog hovered in place, angry but trying to remain calm.

"Mr. Beeba," I said, "let's have some translations here."

"Well," Mr. Beeba said, rising to his feet, "it seems that long ago a feud developed between the Tri-Yarms and the Toogolians. The Tri-Yarms favored a scheme of drawing a limited quantity of glagma from the surface of Toog, just enough to improve their lives a bit. The Toogolians were adamant: Not a drop of glagma was to be touched. Not a drop."

Ragstubble reached into the pot, pulled out another wriggling, wormy thing, and sucked it into his mouth. This time he chewed—slowly, angrily—and swallowed.

Mr. Beeba continued: "That's where Poog's great-uncle comes into the story. We saw a statue of him back on the planet Toog, remember? His name was Zeem."

The mere mention of the name caused Poog to assume a look of deep reverence. Ragstubble made another snorting noise.

"Yeah," I said. "I remember."

"Then you'll recall that when Zeem went to negotiate with the Tri-Yarms, they ambushed him and killed him."

Ragstubble reached out and grabbed my shoulder. "They were looking for a fight! They used Zeem's death as an excuse to wage war on us!"

Poog countered this claim with a high-pitched volley of Toogolian, which brought Ragstubble to his feet again.

"Enough!" I shouted. "Both of you!"

There was silence, apart from the bubbling of the pot.

I motioned Poog away and told Ragstubble to sit down. "Look, forget about the feud. Forget about Poog's great-uncle. This is not about the past. This is about what's going on right now, today. And I'm not going to stand here wasting time while the two of you act like children."

Both Poog and Ragstubble looked offended. Spuckler and Mr. Beeba looked surprised but impressed.

I walked over to where Ragstubble sat and stood in front of him. "Now, listen. We've got problems to deal with. *Big* problems. And Mr. Ragstubble, you've got a choice to make. Are you going to help us save the planet Toog? Or are you going to just sit there eating those disgusting little wormy things? Because if you are, I'm leaving."

Ragstubble narrowed his eyes. He was still chewing.

He looked at me, then Spuckler, then Mr. Beeba and Poog.

He swallowed.

He raised a single finger and shook it at me.

"They're wormy," he said. "But they are *not* disgusting."

Chapter 15

Why did Ragstubble agree to help us? I don't know. Maybe he did it as a favor to Spuckler. Maybe he did it out of love for his old home planet. Maybe he just enjoyed a challenge. One thing's for sure, though. Once he put his mind to defeating the core eater, he was committed, one hundred percent.

He began by passing around bowls of stew and insisting that we swallow every drop. "We've got a lot of work ahead of us," he said. "Can't do it on an empty stomach."

It wasn't as gross as the worm stuff he'd been eating. It was pretty nasty, though, like a mixture of overcooked cabbage and freshly used gym socks. I must have been hungry, because I ate it. I even licked the bowl.

When we were done, Ragstubble took us around to a place behind the shack where a dozen or so spaceships were parked, most of them with their hoods open and engines hanging out. The one he led us to was a big egg-shaped thing that was covered—and I mean *completely* covered—in armor. There wasn't even a windshield, just a little glass hole about the size of a dime.

"This'll get us past the drobe mines," Ragstubble said. "She can withstand more than a hundred hits and still keep going." He opened a door and invited us in.

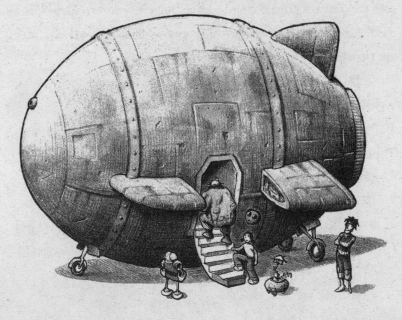

It was cramped inside. *Really* cramped. The walls were about fifteen feet thick all the way around, which didn't leave much legroom for passengers. "Don't be afraid to rub elbows, now," Ragstubble said. "We're all friends here, right?" He thought a bit and added in a half whisper, "Well, *most* of us are, anyway."

Moments later we were up in the air and out among the stars. Not that I could *see* any stars, since there weren't any windows. But Ragstubble kept us informed of our progress toward Toog, peering out the single glass eye in the front of the ship.

"So whaddaya think, Fluggs?" said Spuckler. "How are we gonna sneak inside this baby?" He was studying a blueprint Ragstubble had given him of the inner workings of a core eater.

"Trust me, Spuck," Ragstubble said. "I got it all worked out."

Spuckler turned to me and grinned, as if to say, "See? What'd I tell ya?"

An hour passed.

Then another.

Finally we arrived back on the planet Toog. Poog told Ragstubble where the core eater was. It was the first thing Poog had said to him since they'd blown up at each other back in Ragstubble's shack. His voice was cold, businesslike. I guess Poog had resigned himself to working with a Tri-Yarm, but that didn't mean he had to be happy about the idea.

Ragstubble followed Poog's directions and got us back to the valley we'd fled not so long ago. We were soon within a mile of the core eater.

"Ya might wanna brace yourselves," said Ragstubble, with all the concern of someone advising you to watch your head as you went down the stairs. "Here come the drobe mines."

He made no adjustment to the course we were flying. His plan—as far as I could tell—was to simply plow through the mines as if they weren't even there.

But they were there. They were *definitely* there.

FLUMP! FLUMP! FLOMP! FLUMP!

The first mines hit us with no more effect than snowballs hitting a tank. The sound was muffled, and the ship hardly vibrated at all.

"Man!" said Spuckler. "I gotta get *me* one of these vee-hicles."

Ragstubble patted the dashboard affectionately.

"She's a real beaut, isn't she?"

FLA-FLUMP! FLA-FLOMP!

FLA-FLUM-FLUM-FLUMP!

The drobe mines started hitting with greater frequency. Some of them caused more of a vibration than others. Mr. Beeba began to hum quietly.

"Don't worry," said Ragstubble, looking through the glass eye. "We're almost there."

BUDDA-BUNK! BUDDA-BUNK!

The interior of the ship was heating up. Gax twitched nervously, and Poog looked troubled. Ragstubble was hunched over the dashboard: tensed, pushing buttons, making calculations. "Man," he said. "Sure are a *lot* of 'em."

BUDDA-BUNK! BUDDA-BUDDA-BUNK!

The ship was beginning to creak under the barrage of drobe mine hits. Sweat rolled down my cheeks. Spuckler turned and gave me a wink that was probably meant to be reassuring. "Almost there, 'Kiko." He put a hand on Ragstubble's shoulder. "Right, Fluggs?"

Ragstubble didn't bother to answer. I'm not sure he even heard the question.

BUDDA-BUDDA-BUNK! BUDDA-BUDDA-BUNK!

"I never seen so many drobe mines in all my life!" Ragstubble sounded like a sea captain in the thick of a storm. "There's *thousands* of 'em!"

Now the ship was rattling like crazy. Smoke was seeping out of cracks and crevices in the walls, and dials on the dashboard were spinning out of control. Mr. Beeba began to whimper uncontrollably.

I couldn't take it anymore. "Get us out of here!" I cried. "You're going to get us all killed!"

"It's too late for that!" Ragstubble shouted. "We're goin' down!"

BUDDA-BUDDA-BUDDA
 BUDDA-BUDDA-BUDDA

The drobe mines were slamming into us so regularly it was like a long, low roll of thunder. I could feel the ship falling, tailspinning, plummeting through the air.

FLA-DUMMMPPP!

We hit the ground hard, bounced once, flipped, and hit the ground for good. The drobe mines continued slamming into the ship: The noise rose to a deafening roar as they struck every exposed surface, creating a tooth-chattering tremor that I thought would rattle my eyeballs right out of their sockets.

We all clung to one another and waited.

And waited.

And . . .

   . . . then . . .

      . . . gradually . . .

         . . . the noise started dying down.

The thumps and flumps and fwams and flams began to be interrupted by brief intervals of silence. The ship stopped shaking. Before long I could count the seconds between hits. And after a minute or so . . .

. . . the hits stopped altogether.

Inside, everything was blue with smoke. Alarms bleated and lights flashed. Ragstubble turned from the dashboard and grinned.

"That's it," he said. "We outlasted 'em."

Mr. Beeba—who, to his credit, hadn't fainted—let out the longest, loudest sigh I'd ever heard.

GRA-JUNK!

Ragstubble opened a door, and we all crawled out into the snow. Or what was left of the snow, I should say. The ship was now surrounded by a field of smoking drobe mines—thousands of them—which had melted a circle in the snow about three hundred feet wide. The outside of the ship was covered with them too, making it look like a big burned beehive. But none of this was what I was staring at.

I was looking up.

Directly up.

Because now we were standing in the very shadow of the core eater. There it was, its main body hundreds of feet above, its enormous legs surrounding us like a circle of gigantic mechanical trees. It was making a sort of slow chugging sound but was otherwise surprisingly quiet.

Poog was the first to speak. He had a weird look in his eyes: half pain, half disbelief.

"Heavens," Mr. Beeba said. "They've already made it to the glagma."

I spun around and looked where Mr. Beeba was

pointing. A long flexible tube—the size and length of a railway train—connected the core eater to the ground about half a mile away from us. Every minute or so the tube would swell up at the base, creating a big black muscle that rose from the ground to the core eater, not slowly, not quickly, but steadily, steadily. As soon as one bulge disappeared above, another formed below to take its place.

The death of the planet Toog had already begun.

Chapter 16

"C'mon," said Spuckler as he grabbed Gax and trotted off toward one of the core eater's legs. "Let's get inside this sucker and find out who's sittin' at the controls!"

By the time the rest of us caught up with him, he had already taken a blowtorch out of Gax's innards and was preparing to burn a hole in the surface of the core eater.

Ragstubble snatched the torch out of Spuckler's hands. "Are you some kind of a nutcase? This thing isn't going to do anything but blow our cover!" He chucked it off into the snow, producing groans from both Spuckler and Gax.

"Watch this," said Ragstubble. "I'll show you how to sneak into a core eater."

He walked around to the other side of the core eater's leg and began to climb it.

"He is, you know," Mr. Beeba whispered to me.

"What?"

"Mr. Ragstubble asked if Spuckler was some kind of a nutcase," Mr. Beeba said. "I just thought someone should answer his question, that's all."

Ragstubble was already about twenty feet above us. "What are you waiting for? Follow me!"

We all began climbing after him, pulling ourselves higher and higher by grasping bolts, pipes, and other bits of metal jutting out from the surface. Poog floated alongside us, and Gax carried himself up using the same suction-cup legs he'd used on the Great Wall of Trudd. Before long we reached the first of the two joints that held the leg sections together, about a hundred feet above the ground. Then the second, a hundred more feet up. And finally we arrived at a ledge not far from the body of the core eater itself. Ragstubble encouraged us all to rest and prepare ourselves for what was to come.

"See that ventilation unit over there? That's where we're headed." He was pointing at something about a dozen yards away that jutted down from the surrounding steel like an oversized ceiling lamp. It had large square grills on its sides for bringing air into the core eater.

"I see it, all right," Mr. Beeba said. "But I certainly *don't* see how we're going to get from here to there."

"Ah," said Ragstubble. "That's the fun part."

He removed a small rifle-like tool from his belt, aimed it, and fired.

*FWIZZZZZZZZZZZ*zzzzzzzz

                                   TWUNK!

In the blink of an eye, Ragstubble had anchored a thirty-foot cord to a spot on the underside of the core eater exactly halfway between where we were and where we wanted to be.

"See ya," he said as he leaped off the ledge and swung, Tarzan style, down and across to the ventilation unit. He made it look as easy as a ballerina doing a pirouette. Once he'd found a spot to plant his legs, he sent the cord swinging back to us.

Spuckler chuckled. "I love this guy."

"Wow," I said. "Now, *that* was cool."

Beeba groaned. "Akiko, we are three hundred feet above the ground, with no safety net of any kind. *Cool* is hardly the word. *Crazy* is more li—"

"Show time, Beebs." Spuckler grabbed the cord in one hand and Mr. Beeba's leg in the other . . .

"Noooooooo!"

. . . and leaped wildly into the air. Spuckler (right side up) and Mr. Beeba (upside down and wriggling spastically) cut a surprisingly graceful arc through the air before . . .

THUNK!

. . . Mr. Beeba smacked his head right into the bottom of the ventilation unit.

"Yyyyoooowwwwwrrrch!"

"Keep it down, Beebs," said Spuckler as he hoisted Mr. Beeba up to safety. "You're gonna give us away."

"You—"

Spuckler slapped his hands over Mr. Beeba's mouth just in time to turn the word *idiot* into a muffled *"ibi-ubb!"*

Gax was next, but he had no need for the cord. He just used his suction-cup legs to walk upside down

across the surface of the core eater. Poog and I were the only ones left.

"Get ready, 'Kiko," Spuckler called out. "I'm gonna toss the cord over to ya!"

"Don't bother! I don't need it!"

Spuckler and Ragstubble looked at each other like they thought I'd flipped my lid.

"Come on, Poog," I said, reaching over and placing my hands on top of his head. "Let's show 'em how it's done."

Poog smiled as he braced himself to support my weight.

Then . . .

. . . slowly . . .

. . . Poog carried me out into the air.

We floated over to the others, sailing as smoothly and silently as a swan gliding across a pond.

Mr. Beeba rubbed his head and sighed. "Now, why didn't I think of that?"

"Personally," said Ragstubble, "I think you're better

115

off not depending too much on a Toogolian. They turn on ya when the going gets tough."

Poog glared at Ragstubble but said nothing. I decided to let the comment pass.

Now we were all in position, ready to enter the core eater. The grill, minus half a dozen screws, was open on its hinges like a swinging door for a giant cat. One by one we slipped inside.

Chapter 17

The interior of the core eater was almost pitch-black. Ragstubble drew a small lamp from his side and lit it, while Spuckler switched on Gax's torch and turned it up as bright as it would go. This helped us see where we were going, but it didn't make the place any less spooky.

The vent we had stepped into was like a shallow pit we had to climb out of. Just above it was a narrow passageway that twisted this way and that, forcing us to crawl over enormous pipes and duck under masses of tubes and wires that hung from the ceiling. It felt as if we had snuck into the basement of a darkened factory after hours.

DOO-GUNK
   DOO-GUNK
    DOO-GUNK

A deep pulsing sound vibrated through the walls: pumps drawing the glagma up from Toog's core. A smoky chemical stench hung in the air, and some sort of warm liquid kept dripping from the ceiling, getting in my hair and making nasty unexpected puddles here and there on the floor.

Ragstubble led us on and on, around corners, up steep inclines, and through gaps so narrow we had to turn Gax sideways and shove him through with all our might. "Gotta get to the control room," said Ragstubble. "In the very center of the core eater. Spuck," he added without turning around, "hand me that blueprint, will ya?"

"Blueprint?"

"Yeah. The one you were looking at. Back in the ship."

"I thought *you* had it."

Ragstubble gritted his teeth and made an ugly noise.

"Isn't it wonderful," Mr. Beeba said to me with a smile, "to see Spuckler driving someone *else* crazy?"

There was a loud bang as Ragstubble kicked something, hard, and resumed the journey forward. "Okay. This is *not* a problem. I know core eaters like the back of my hand."

Ragstubble took us up a creaky black ladder and into a passage with a ceiling so low we had to crawl on our hands and knees. Halfway through, I felt an insect land on my leg, crawl over my back, and jump to the floor. Eeeew. It skittered in front of me and climbed over the others in pretty much the same way. When it got to Ragstubble, I saw him snatch it off his leg and pinch it between his fingers.

"A funga-pede. My lucky day." He popped it in his mouth and swallowed it whole.

I wished I hadn't seen that.

At the end of our long, low crawl we came to a small room with a grate in the floor. Peeking through, we saw another vast room below, as big as a football field.

DOO-GUNK

  DOO-GUNK

    DOO-GUNK

It was an engine room.

DOO-GUNK

  DOO-GUNK

    DOO-GUNK

And marching back and forth between the engines . . .
DOO-GUNK
 DOO-GUNK
  DOO-GUNK
"*Tri-Yarms!*"

Spuckler was the only one who dared to say it out loud.

But there was no doubt about it. Every one of the workers in that room was a Tri-Yarm, just like Fluggly Ragstubble.

So that's who's behind all this.

"Impossible," said Ragstubble, his brow twisted in disbelief.

It was possible, all right. Now that I thought about it . . . come on, it was obvious! They were the ones who'd wanted to get at the glagma *years* ago. Ragstubble had never denied that.

Poog was furious. He blurted out something in Toogolian, and Ragstubble gurgled right back at him. It took all of us to force the two of them apart.

"All right all right all right," I said. "So Tri-Yarms are the ones running this core eater."

Ragstubble looked desperate. Like he wanted it to be some kind of big optical illusion.

"It's . . . disappointing," I said. "But it doesn't mean we turn against our friends, does it?"

Poog still looked angry, but he had calmed down a little.

" 'Kiko's right," Spuckler said, placing a firm hand on Ragstubble's shoulder. "This don't change nothin'. We came here to get the bad guys, and the bad guys're who we're goin' after. Not you, Fluggs."

"Absolutely," Mr. Beeba said. "We mustn't descend into the murky muck of finger-pointing and declarations of guilt by association." Ragstubble smiled appreciatively. "Not that the *concept* of guilt by association is entirely without *merit* . . ."

"Thanks, Mr. Beeba," I said. "Great insight there. Let's keep going."

So on we went.

But even though Spuckler claimed it didn't change anything . . .

. . . it did.

It made me wonder, just a little, whose side our Tri-Yarm friend was really on.

Chapter 18

Ragstubble led us away from the grate and took us to another rickety ladder. This one went up and up for at least fifty feet. When we reached the top, Ragstubble pulled out some tools and began picking a lock in a portal above his head.

"If I've done my job, this should put us in a hallway just outside the control room," he said. "Gax, come up here for a second, will ya?"

Gax, *zupping* and *zopping* on his suction-cup legs, climbed the wall and positioned himself next to Ragstubble's shoulder.

"Stick your peep-eye up through this crack and see if the coast is clear."

Gax opened a compartment on his side and stretched out a spindly mechanical tube tipped with a tiny electronic eye. He made it snake this way and that until it had wormed its way through a hole in the portal.

"TRI-YARM SENTRIES. THEY'RE WELL ARMED." He waited a moment, then added, "IF YOU'LL EXCUSE THE PUN."

Everyone groaned. (Everyone, that is, except Spuckler, who apparently didn't get the joke.)

"How many?" I asked.

Gax twisted the mechanical tube back and forth, counting.

"TEN. NINE COMMON SENTRIES AND ONE MASTER SENTRY."

There was a pause. All eyes turned to Ragstubble.

"Well, Fluggs," Spuckler said. "Whaddaya think? How're we gonna get past these guys?"

I watched Ragstubble's face. This was it. If we wanted a test to see whose side he was on, we were about to get it.

He smiled. "You guys are lucky I'm here."

"Why?" I asked.

"Because it takes a Tri-Yarm . . . ," he replied, slipping a black gas mask over his nose and mouth, "to *fool* a Tri-Yarm."

Throwing the portal open wide, he crawled up and into the corridor above us, casually, noisily even. He winked at me before slamming the portal shut behind him.

No way. Is he going to do battle with ten Tri-Yarms all by himself?

"What the—" we heard one of the Tri-Yarm guards say.

"Hoh boy!" Ragstubble's voice, loud and tired-sounding, echoed down to us through the portal. "When they said this place needed repairs, they weren't kiddin'!"

Spuckler grinned. "Fluggs," he whispered to me. "What an actor."

"Repairs?" It was a different Tri-Yarm voice this time.

"What, they didn't tell ya?" Ragstubble said.

A third Tri-Yarm voice joined the discussion, this one very authoritative. He must have been the boss of the others. "There was no mention of repairs in this morning's meeting."

"Obviously not," said Ragstubble. "None of ya are wearin' gas masks." Spuckler clamped a hand over his mouth. He'd have been howling with laughter otherwise.

"Look, Mr., uh . . . ," the boss voice began.

"Kogg-Nito," Ragstubble said. "Of Kogg-Nito's Core Eater Service and Repair. All makes, all models. Open twenty-four hours. You nix it up, we fix it up. . . ."

"Mr. Kogg-Nito," the boss voice said, "just what exactly is going on here?" He sounded suspicious, but also just a little nervous.

"Only a gluco-cyanide leak in this whole dang corridor, that's all." Ragstubble made a *tut-tut-tut*ting sound. "Jeez. They really didn't *tell* you, did they? That's criminal."

"Gluco-cyanide?" two of the guards said at once.

"Oh yeah. The air is practically dripping with it up here. I can't believe you're all still alive."

"Now, hold on here," the boss voice said. "I don't smell anything."

"Buddy, didn't ya ever go to grade school? Gluco-cyanide is odorless. You'll drop dead before you *smell* anything." Spuckler slapped a second hand over his mouth and squirmed with delight.

"Boss," said one of the guards, "maybe we should, uh, go on break until they've finished the repairs."

"Now, *there's* an idea," said Ragstubble. "And while you're at it, you better getcher butts down to the mess hall, where they're handin' out gas masks. With all the GC you guys've been breathin', I figure you already got a fifty-fifty chance of kickin' the bucket as it is. . . ."

There was a clattering of boots as several of the guards trotted away, presumably heading toward the mess hall.

"Hey!" the boss voice bellowed. "I didn't say you could go on break!" Several more pairs of boots clattered off.

"You'll all get docked pay for this!"

Off went another pair or two.

"And, and . . . no more bathroom privileges!"

Soon the only voices left were those of the boss and Ragstubble. Problem was, the boss was not about to leave.

"Now, I admire that," Ragstubble said. "A guy who

won't leave his post even if it means a slow, painful death. Not to mention the intestinal bleeding."

"I'm not leaving," the boss said. "Someone has to stay behind and protect the entrance to the control room."

"I do admire that," said Ragstubble. "I really do."

A long silence followed. Spuckler was no longer smiling.

I figured Ragstubble would keep trying to get rid of the guy, but all he did was start whistling.

Gax, who still had his electronic eye poking through the portal, told us what was going on.

"MR. RAGSTUBBLE HAS TURNED HIS BACK TO THE MASTER SENTRY. HE'S INSPECTING A THERMOSTAT ON THE WALL."

"C'mon, Fluggs," Spuckler whispered. "Time's a-wastin'."

The silence stretched on.

It was the boss, not Ragstubble, who finally spoke up.

"Uh, Mr. Kogg-Nito," he said in a hushed voice, "I don't suppose you have an . . . extra gas mask *on* you?"

"Oh yeah. I do, I do," said Ragstubble. "Here, let me get it for you. . . ."

FWUP

ZWIT

SSSWOOT

The sounds of a skirmish. Then:

PAAAASSSHH!

The portal rattled as something heavy landed right on top of it. Gax retracted his mechanical arm just in time.

sssssssssssshhhhhhhhhhh

The sound of something heavy being dragged across the floor.

Silence.

Then the portal was yanked open and there in front of us was Ragstubble's face: smiling, triumphant.

"The coast is clear."

Yes!

We all climbed out and assembled in the middle of the corridor, just in front of the entrance to the control room. Ragstubble had removed a key from the guard's belt and was looking for the keyhole. It wasn't right next to the door, where you'd expect it, but was hidden somewhere nearby.

Poog said something. Quietly, but with the tone of someone giving an order.

"Poog says he wants it understood," said Mr. Beeba, "that *he* will be the one to deal with the Tri-Yarm leader. He advises the rest of us to stand back and keep out of the way."

"Is he going to . . . *brainmelt* him?" I asked.

Ragstubble flinched at the very mention of the word.

"No," Mr. Beeba said. "He's going to do what's known as a brain*pierce*. Highly effective on Tri-Yarms. It will render him docile, powerless, incapable of violence. But it won't kill him."

I breathed a sigh of relief. I didn't know if I could handle seeing a Tri-Yarm with brains oozing out of his ears.

"Found it, Fluggs." Spuckler had located the keyhole inside a light fixture on the wall opposite the door. "C'mon. Let's get in there so Poog can do his brain-stabbin' thing and we can all go home."

K'CHAK

Ragstubble slid the key into the keyhole.

FSSHHZZZZzzzzz

The control-room door rose into the ceiling, revealing a short, dimly lit passageway. At the end was a large

circular room filled with monitors, switchboards, and
rows and rows of buttons, lights, and levers.

Poog led the way. He floated through the passageway and into the control room. As nervous as I was, I
didn't want to miss the look on the Tri-Yarm leader's

face when he saw Poog, so I made sure I was as near to the front of the group as I could get. Before I made it even halfway down the passageway, I sensed that something was wrong.

It was Poog.

The look on his face.

He was shocked. Stunned. Speechless.

I took the last few steps to the end of the passageway and poked my head around the corner.

There, in the center of the room, smiling, fearless, reflecting everything in his big, glassy eyes . . .

"*Zeem!*" cried Mr. Beeba.

Chapter 19

Zeem? Poog's great-uncle?

But he was supposed to be *dead!*

"Well, well, well," a creaky, crackly voice said, *"if it isn't Poog. My very favorite . . . distant blood relation . . ."*

It took a second to make out where the voice was coming from. Then I saw it: a gray-black slimy growth attached to the back of Zeem's head. It had jointed legs like a tarantula, a bulbous body, and, at the end of its long spindly neck, a tiny toothless mouth.

"A tongue-leech," said Mr. Beeba. "It allows its host to speak in any language he desires."

"Poog, my boy," the voice continued, its words coming out in slurred clusters, *"you really should have told me you*

were . . . *coming to visit. Especially if you planned to bring . . . so many friends."*

Listening carefully, I realized that Zeem's tongue-leech was speaking in a multitude of languages all at once, Toogolian included. I was somehow able to hear only the language I understood best.

Poog was silent. His earlier look of dismay had twisted itself into a furious scowl.

"What's Poog going to do?" I asked.

"What, indeed. A brainpierce would be useless," Mr. Beeba whispered. "Toogolians are immune to it."

Poog floated forward until he was just a foot or two from his great-uncle. He said something in Toogolian: He was quiet, but smoldering with anger.

I noticed, for the first time, Zeem's mouth. It was sealed shut from disuse, like a scar that had never really healed.

It was revolting.

When he smiled, it was even worse.

"I don't need to justify my actions to you, Poog. Don't act like you're . . . any more dedicated to this planet than I am." The tongue-leech's lips moved up and down, up and down. *"How are your meditations going, by the way?"* An ugly little smile.

Poog flinched. He was still angry, but a bit of fear had crept into his face.

"Now, I have some . . . advice for you, little one," Zeem's tongue-leech said to Poog. "Take your friends . . . and leave this place at once."

Poog stayed exactly where he was.

Zeem moved forward until his eyes and Poog's eyes were just inches apart. "Don't cross me, Poog. I have powers you can't begin to imagine. Powers the other elders . . . haven't even scratched the surface of."

If Poog was frightened, he didn't show it.

He closed his eyes.

Said a few words.

And slowly . . .

. . . out of thin air . . .

. . . a cage began to form around Zeem.

It was transparent at first; then bit by bit it gathered substance. Zeem watched without emotion as the cage completed itself. It glowed pale blue, sometimes shimmering with electricity, as if it were made from frozen bolts of lightning.

When it was finished, Poog opened his eyes.

"A mind-snare," Mr. Beeba whispered. "Perfect. Virtually indestructible."

Zeem's mouth smiled.

"Is that the best you can do? How disappointing."

SPAAASH!

The cage disintegrated into shards of blue light, then vanished altogether.

"Let's not play children's games, Poog." The tongue-leech's voice was shrill with impatience. *"If you wish to do battle with me properly . . . then do so. If not, go. Go. Be gone. Before someone . . . gets . . ."*

A long, long pause.

"*. . . damaged.*"

I wanted to believe Poog would defeat his great-uncle. Wanted to. *Really* wanted to.

Poog closed his eyes again. He tensed up, quivered, as if he was summoning up every last scrap of energy he had.

He said a word or two in Toogolian.

Gradually the room filled with light.

Poog had conjured a ghostly green whirlpool of clouds. It appeared in the air just behind Zeem and quickly grew until it filled more than half the room.

Zeem began to be sucked into the whirlpool. A look of panic overtook his face as he was drawn inch by inch into the glowing green hole.

"This will do it!" Mr. Beeba cried. "It's a Toogolian detention vortex. It'll take Zeem in and hold him for as long as—"

But Zeem was already laughing through his tongue-leech lips.

The look of panic had been a fake.

The whirlpool was having no effect on him whatso-
ever.

ZOOOOOOSSSH!

All at once the green clouds evaporated, leaving
Zeem just as he was and Poog panting for air, utterly
exhausted.

"Enough of this mucking about." Zeem closed his eyes—
briefly, little more than a blink—and his tongue-leech
spat out a few short words, this time in Toogolian only.

Instantly an enormous block of yellowish ice
formed around Poog, trapping him like a fly in amber.
He was locked up, motionless, a confused expression
frozen on his face.

Zeem chuckled and turned to the rest of us.

"Well, he tried, *didn't he? I'll give him that much."*

I stared in horror at Poog. I stared for as long as I
could take it. Then I turned away and tried not to start
bawling.

Zeem's face settled into an angry glare.

"Anyone else?"

Chapter 20

I looked at Ragstubble. He seemed to have a very clear idea of what we were up against. He must have known that any move he made would be pointless. So he made no move.

Spuckler, on the other hand . . .

"All right, Zeemy!" Spuckler had stepped forward with clenched fists, as if he intended to challenge Zeem to a round of boxing. "Enough of this flim-flam-alakazaam business. I'm gonna duke it out with ya the old-fashioned way."

Ragstubble shook his head. "Stand back, Spuck. You don't know what you're messin' with here."

"I reckon you're right about that, Fluggs," said

Spuckler. "But I ain't goin' down without a fight."

Zeem chuckled. *"Humanoids."* Even as he spoke, Spuckler's hand began to quiver. *"Silly little things."*

One of Spuckler's arms began to move through the air: away from Zeem, down, over, down, over.

"Very silly. And yet . . . they do have their uses."

Spuckler was now on his knees, one hand reaching up behind Gax's head.

"PLEASE, SIR . . ."

"It's . . ." Spuckler's eyes were wide with disbelief. ". . . It's not me, Gax! It's movin' by itself!"

Before anyone could do anything . . .

B'CHAK!

Gax's neck shuddered, then fell limp, sending his robot head and helmet crashing to the floor. Now Gax was as motionless as Poog.

"My word," Mr. Beeba said. "He . . . shut Gax down."

Spuckler had a strangely blank expression on his face. Like he refused to believe he'd done what he'd done. Mr. Beeba was quivering behind me like a frightened dog. I was hardly any more composed than he was. Only Ragstubble remained strong and defiant.

He said something to Zeem in Toogolian: The tone of his voice was angry, but there was a hint of pleading in it.

"Very valiant of you, Tri-Yarm," replied Zeem. *"But no. What good would it do me to brainmelt you and let everyone else go?"*

I swallowed hard.

"The truth is I'm not very fond of brainmelting," said Zeem. *"So messy. And a waste of warm bodies. We Toogolians . . . need all the arms and legs we can get, you know. I think I'll just brainpierce you for the moment. Then later on we can see about turning you all into my slaves."*

Ragstubble started to say something.

Zeem didn't let him finish. *"Enough!"* He closed his eyes and opened his tongue-leech mouth. Toogolian words came gurgling out.

Ragstubble. Spuckler. Mr. Beeba. They all dropped

to the floor, still breathing but as motionless as rag dolls. Their eyes stayed open but turned glassy and expressionless, like the eyes of fish.

I was the only one left standing.

Zeem stared at me in astonishment.

"Impressive" was all he said at first. He floated forward and circled me. *"Resistant to brainpiercing. Most unexpected."* He circled me again. *"You do have a brain, little girl, don't you?"*

I was too scared to speak. Too horrified that there was no one left to defend me but *me*.

Zeem stopped circling.

"Well, now. Let's try brainmelting, then."

He closed his eyes. Gurgled some words. Opened his eyes again.

I stood there. I had no idea what was going on. But one thing was sure: My brain was as unmelted as it had always been.

Zeem was stunned.

He closed his eyes and uttered a few more words.

Nothing.

He closed his eyes again and again, gurgled one set of words, then another, and another.

Nothing happened to me. Nothing at all.

Zeem was now gazing at me with a look of deep admiration.

"Astonishing. I can't freeze you. I can't burn you. I can't turn you to stone. I can't make your skin fall off or your head turn inside out. I can't even give you a mild temperature. You . . . are immune to Toogolian brain warfare."

Chapter 21

Let's face it. Whatever was protecting me from Zeem was a real miracle. I should have been dancing for joy. But something—I think it was the way Zeem was looking at me—made me feel more frightened than ever.

"This is a welcome development," he said. *"A stroke of good luck."*

He began circling again.

"Look at you. A harmless little girl. And yet impervious to the destructive powers of a Toogolian master. You'll be handy to have around . . . when it comes to dealing with other would-be Toogolian heroes."

He began to circle faster.

"Perfect, perfect. We'll be a team, you and I. And to think you were delivered to me by my enemies. That . . . that's really a delicious bit of irony, isn't it?"

He kept talking, circling, talking. I felt like a bug in a web.

Think, I told myself. Think.

There had to be something I could do. Something I could at least try.

Zeem circled, circled, spinning plans for me, talking about things I would do for him, uses I could be put to.

If only I had something to defend myself with. Some sort of weapon. But I had nothing. Well, okay, not nothing. I had a nickel in my pocket. That and the package of bubble gum I'd bought at Chuck's way back before this whole mess got started.

Bubble gum! Ha! Some weapon.

But wait.

Bubble gum . . .

An idea came to me.

I reached into my pocket and pulled out the package of Dr. Yubble's Ooey-Gooey Double-Trouble Bubble Gum.

Zeem circled. By this point he was too wrapped up in his crazy schemes to pay me any mind.

There were seven pieces of gum left. One by one I unwrapped them and popped them into my mouth.

One, two, three . . .

The sugar! Man, that stuff was sweet.

. . . four, five, six . . .

And gooey. *Very* gooey. Much gooier than it had been on Earth. Maybe there was some sort of extra goo factor that came from passing through Toog's atmosphere. Or else just from having been skwunched up in my pocket for so long.

. . . seven.

My mouth was now so packed with bubble gum I could barely breathe. Which made me happy. That was exactly what I wanted from that gum.

Zeem circled.

I chewed.

Zeem circled.

I had to face facts: There'd be only one chance to do what I wanted to do. One chance. If I blew it, Zeem would just call in some of his Tri-Yarm goons and have them cart me away.

Zeem circled.

I chewed.

I was waiting for the perfect time to make my move. The problem with waiting for a perfect time is that you always end up telling yourself you should wait a little longer, for a time that's a little more perfect.

Zeem circled.

I chewed.

Unfortunately, I had been so busy thinking about my plan that I'd stopped listening to what Zeem was saying. Otherwise, I'd have noticed that he'd gradually convinced himself he didn't really want me around after all.

"*Yes, yes, sad but true,*" the tongue-leech was saying when I finally focused again. "*I can't work with a creature of such immunities. Who knows what other powers she has? It's simply not worth the risk.*" He stopped circling and looked at me. "*Yes. I'll call in some Tri-Yarms and have them get rid of her.*"

This was it. The time—perfect or not—was now.

I quietly spat the bubble gum into my left hand.

It was the size of a large plum. Heavy. Sticky.

"*Sorry, child,*" Zeem said to me, not looking sorry at all. "*You'll have to be dealt with in a somewhat more brutal fashion than your friends were. Don't worry, though. I'll tell them to execute you quickly, so as to minimize the pai—*"

I lunged forward and grabbed Zeem's tongue-leech by its neck.

It took no more than a second.

Gum in hand . . .

   . . . I shoved my arm . . .

      . . . down the leech's throat . . .

         . . . down, down, deep down . . .

            . . . as far as I possibly could.

For an awful half-second my entire left arm was trapped inside the tongue-leech's warm, slimy throat. I let go of the gum and yanked my arm out.

ZZLLLUUUURRRP!

Ugh! I dropped to the floor and watched as Zeem's tongue-leech wriggled and writhed, trying frantically to dislodge the sticky gob of gum from its throat. But it was stuck down there, and stuck good: The Double-Trouble gum was living up to its name.

Zeem's eyes bugged out. His eyelids fluttered, then drooped.

The tongue-leech began to move more slowly. The two of them descended to the floor. As they touched bottom, I saw the tongue-leech detach itself from Zeem and shrivel up like a dying spider; it grew utterly still, dead still, and Zeem . . . well, he looked like he was in serious pain. Like he'd just had a vital organ removed. He rolled on the floor, quietly moaning to himself.

That was when I heard a gurgling noise behind me.

Please, no. Not another Toogolian.

I whirled around. It *was* another Toogolian.

My own personal favorite Toogolian, that is.

Poog.

Chapter 22

The yellow ice trap had vanished. Poog was alive and well. Not only that, but all the others—Spuckler, Mr. Beeba, and Ragstubble—had snapped out of Zeem's brainpiercing spell. I guess as Zeem got weaker, the effects of his Toogolian mind tricks wore off.

"Lordy, 'Kiko!" said Spuckler, inspecting the limp, lifeless body of the tongue-leech. "What'd ya *do* to it?"

I explained exactly what I'd done. I even told them a little about Chuck's, just to make sure they got the big picture.

"Very clever, Akiko," said Mr. Beeba. "How did you know Zeem had become dependent on his tongue-leech? That hurting one would hurt the other?"

"I didn't. I just figured it was worth a shot, that's all."

Mr. Beeba examined the huge lump in the tongue-leech's throat. The rest of the creature had shriveled up so much, the lump looked very big by comparison. "Remarkable," said Mr. Beeba. "I'd always suspected chewing gum wasn't good for you, but good heavens!"

Ragstubble was already working the control panels of the core eater, switching things off, killing power generators, shutting down the whole monstrous operation. As he did, I could hear the sound of the pumps—faint, but always there in the background—die down and come to a complete halt.

"Gimme a couple minutes here," said Ragstubble. "I think there's a way of reversing the glagma flow. Might as well get it all back down there where it belongs."

Poog smiled. If he'd ever had doubts about Ragstubble's motives, they were completely gone now. So were mine.

Spuckler turned his attention to Gax. It took a minute or two—and a lot of popping and sputtering—but soon he had Gax up and running again. It was such a relief to see him moving his head around and scooting back and forth!

Mr. Beeba and Poog were huddled around Zeem. Poog had coated him in some sort of healing orange glow. Mr. Beeba said it would keep Zeem alive but never allow him to cause anyone harm again.

I sat and listened as Poog spoke to Mr. Beeba in spirited gurgles, trying to piece together the puzzle of how Toog's greatest hero had turned into such a greedy glagma thief.

"An excellent theory, Poog," Mr. Beeba said. "I'll bet that's precisely how it happened."

"How what happened?" I asked.

"Well, Poog suspects it all started years and years ago when Zeem first proposed his mission to negotiate with the Tri-Yarms. He must have had his eyes on the glagma even then. So he went to some of the more unscrupulous Tri-Yarm leaders and converted them to his way of thinking. Then he enlisted their help in faking his own death."

"But why go to so much trouble to make people think he was dead? Why not just go straight for the glagma?"

"His main interest at that stage was in starting a war between the Toogolians and the Tri-Yarms. He knew that word of his being senselessly murdered would be just the thing to set the Toogolians off. He wanted all the Tri-Yarms driven off the planet. That way when he returned, core eater in tow, he'd have all the glagma to himself and not have to share it with anyone. Well, no one but his small core of Tri-Yarm followers."

"Wow, he must have really wanted that glagma."

Mr. Beeba shook his head slowly. "He wanted more than just glagma, Akiko. He wanted to become an entirely different sort of life-form."

"He *what*?"

"I know. It's very odd. But you see, simply put, Zeem hated being a Toogolian. It was a part of his character that very few people knew about. Poog had observed it on occasion but never imagined it would drive him to such lengths."

Mr. Beeba now turned to Zeem, regarding him with an expression of both pity and mystification.

"He wanted to be bigger, stronger, to have capabilities that had always been denied him as a Toogolian. The tongue-leech was just the first part of the process. It gave him the sophisticated vocal cords that Toogolians lack. It also gave him deadly powers, powers beyond those of ordinary Toogolians."

I thought about this.

"That tongue-leech gave *me* something too."

Mr. Beeba looked puzzled. "*You?* What did it give you?"

"The creeps."

Mr. Beeba snorted. "You and me both."

Ragstubble brushed his hands together like a workman at the end of the day. "There we go. This here glagma-thieving operation is now officially over. Let's get out of here!"

"Great," I said. "But how? The ship we came here in is wrecked, and the police car ship is on a whole different planet."

Spuckler chuckled. "'Kiko, all the transport we need is right here under our feet." He turned to Ragstubble. "C'mon, Fluggs. Show her how it's done."

"Next stop," Ragstubble said, punching a few buttons and getting into a driver's seat on one side of the room, "Shring-la Rai!"

Chapter 23

An hour or so later we arrived outside Toog's capital city, lumbering into town the only way the core eater knew how: loudly and menacingly. We must have scared Shring-la Rai's population half to death. But once Poog went in and explained things to the Toogolian elders, word got around that a celebration was in order. By the end of the day, Shring-la Rai had transformed itself into a huge outdoor party.

Of course, Toogolians being Toogolians, it wasn't a big crazy blowout like we'd have on Earth. It was mostly very quiet, except for the singing of Toogolians throughout the city, which was as soft as the sound of crickets on a summer evening. At night there was

something Mr. Beeba called a phosphorescence ballet. It was a bunch of glowing balls of light—some as big as buildings, some as small as fireflies—that danced in the sky until the wee hours of the morning, making huge intricate patterns and painting the clouds a hundred different shades of violet, pink, and orange.

The Toogolian elders made three great declarations that day: that all of us were to be guests of honor on Toog for as long as we wished to stay; that those Tri-Yarms who had collaborated with Zeem would be banned from Toog forever; and that innocent Tri-Yarms throughout the universe were free to return to the planet Toog at once if they so desired, with a promise that amends would be made for all the injustices against them in the past.

Toward the end of the celebrations, Poog called a special session of the elders, during which he admitted that he had abandoned his meditations and was not the proper Toogolian elder he appeared to be. The other elders voted unanimously that he be completely forgiven for this; they even offered him a higher position as a reward for his services to the planet.

Poog caused quite a stir by turning them down on this last offer, saying he no longer wished to be an elder at all, but just an ordinary Toogolian. He had decided to spend the rest of his life on the planet Smoo, growing old with his friends there and returning to Toog only on special occasions. (The elders promised they would concoct as many special occasions as they could.)

When the celebrations had ended, we all climbed aboard the core eater, and to Spuckler's delight, Ragstubble put its rocket boosters on full throttle, lifting us into the air, up through the clouds, and off into space. A couple of hours later we arrived back on Ragstubble's home planet. It was only when Spuckler got into the spaceship police car and revved up the engine that it suddenly hit me: I was going to have to say goodbye to Ragstubble, and there was no telling when I'd see him again.

"Thanks for everything, Mr. Ragstubble. We'd have never pulled it off without your help."

"Fluggly," he replied. "You gotta call me Fluggly from now on. We're friends, for cryin' out loud."

I smiled. "It's a little late for 'from now on,' isn't it?"

"You kiddin'? I want you back here soon. *Real* soon. Never did sample my skubb eel soup, did ya?"

"You mean the little wormy things?"

"I believe the phrase you used was '*disgusting* little wormy things.'"

"Hey," I said, "I call 'em like I see 'em."

HONK HONK

"C'mon, 'Kiko," Spuckler called from the police car. "Enough already. Long sad goodbyes're for sissies."

I gave old Fluggly a hug and a kiss on his big stubbly cheek and trotted off to begin my flight home. The last I saw of him, as we rose into the air, was a toothy grin and three arms waving goodbye.

During the flight back to Earth I had a nice long chat with Poog and Mr. Beeba.

"That must have been tough for you, Poog, giving up being a Toogolian elder. Are you afraid you might regret it someday?"

Poog shook his head and gurgled cheerfully. "He thinks he was never really cut out for elderhood anyway," Mr. Beeba said. "Too many rules and far too little fun."

"*That's* for dang sure," said Spuckler. "I never *seen* such a buncha tired old party poopers. Stick with me,

Poog. I'll show ya what life's all about: fistfights and Bropka burgers."

Poog smiled, and Mr. Beeba rolled his eyes.

Gax was burning with curiosity about what had happened while he was out of service.

"WHY WASN'T ZEEM ABLE TO BRAINMELT AKIKO?" he said. "OR EVEN BRAINPIERCE HER?"

Poog answered with a question.

"He wants to know if you have something called an appendix," Mr. Beeba said.

"An appendix?"

"It's a small organ in the human body, apparently."

I remembered how a friend of mine at school got appendicitis a few years ago and had to have her appendix removed.

"Well, I've never had mine removed," I said, "so sure, I guess I *must* have an appendix."

Poog gurgled a bit more.

"You're very lucky, Akiko," Mr. Beeba explained. "That appendix of yours is what saved you. It serves as a sort of shield against Toogolian brain warfare. Human beings are among the very few life-forms in the universe that possess such an organ."

"Wow. People on Earth think this thing is useless," I

said, tapping my stomach in what I hoped was the general area of my appendix. "I wish I could tell my science teacher about this."

We arrived back in Middleton on a cool sunny morning and caught up with the Akiko robot strolling along Wabash Avenue. Spuckler guided the ship into a nearby alleyway and we prepared to make the switch. When I saw my backpack slung over the robot's shoulders, I realized that we'd intercepted her on the way to Middleton Elementary for the start of another school day.

"Lousy timing, guys," I said as I opened the back door to get out. "Maybe we can take an extra spin around the galaxy until school's over."

Spuckler and Mr. Beeba looked at each other and chuckled. There was a kind of *Why not?* expression on their faces.

I had one foot outside the car.

"That was a joke," I said.

"I know it was," said Mr. Beeba. "But it doesn't *have* to be."

I looked at the Akiko robot. There was no getting around it. She was a lot more ready for a day at school than I was.

"Hey, c'mon, 'Kiko," Spuckler said. "You just saved

a whole *planet.* If that doesn't entitle ya to a day off, I don't know what does."

"I QUITE AGREE, MA'AM," said Gax. "A BIT MORE REST WOULD DO YOU GOOD."

I pulled my foot back inside the car.

Shut the door.

Folded my arms behind my head.

"You know, I've always wanted to see the rings of Saturn. . . ."

Mr. Beeba smiled.

"Close your eyes," he said. "We'll be there before you know it."

Be sure to read

the exciting new series from

Mark Crilley!

Excerpt from *Billy Clikk: Creatch Battler*
Copyright © 2004 by Mark Crilley
Published by Delacorte Press
an imprint of Random House Children's Books
a division of Random House, Inc.
New York

All rights reserved

CHAPTER 1

SKEETER GIG. BACK LATE, DON'T WAIT UP. DINNER'S IN
THE FUDGE. LOVE, MOM & DAD

Billy Clikk read the Post-it again.

"*Fridge.* She meant fridge." Crumpling up the yellow square, Billy chucked it at the garbage can and watched it fly in and then bounce out onto the kitchen floor. It was the third time this week he'd come home from school to find his parents gone, leaving him to heat leftovers in the microwave, do his homework, and put himself to bed. At this point they could just leave a note reading THE USUAL and he'd know exactly what it meant.

There was an upside, though: Billy was now free to kick back and watch his favorite TV show, *Truly Twisted.* He dashed into the living room, leaped over the couch, grabbed the remote, and switched on the TV.

Truly Twisted was the one program his parents said he must never, never watch. These guys took extreme sports to a whole new level: they once snuck into a church, climbed up the steeple, and bungee-jumped right into the middle of some guy's wedding. It was pretty awesome.

When Billy got to the channel where *Truly Twisted* was supposed to be airing, though, there was nothing more extreme than some lame college tennis championship. "Oh, come on!" Billy cried. They'd bumped the best show on cable for a couple of scrawny guys knocking a ball back and forth.

Billy shut off the TV and slouched back into the kitchen. He yanked open the "fudge," pulled out a brown paper bag, and peeked inside. Cold chicken curry: carryout from the Delhi Deli, an Indian restaurant down the street. Billy used to like their chicken curry. Back before he'd eaten it once or twice a week, every week, for about three years.

Billy pursed his lips, made a farting sound, and tossed the bag back in the refrigerator. He slammed the door a lot harder than he really needed to and stared at the floor. There, next to his foot, sat the crumpled-up Post-it note.

"Are pest problems getting *you* down?" he said, suddenly doing a superdeep TV-commercial voice. "Then you should pick up that phone and call Jim and Linda Clikk, founders of BUGZ-B-GON, the best extermination service in all of Piffling,

Indiana." He leaned down and picked up the wadded note, and as he straightened up, he added a tone of mystery to his voice. The TV commercial had turned into a piece of investigative journalism. "What makes the Clikks so busy? What drives them to spend their every waking hour on extermination jobs— 'skeeter gigs,' as they call them? Is it *really* necessary for them to devote so much of their time and energy to saving total strangers from termites and hornets' nests? Is it just for the money, or is killing bugs some kind of a weird power trip?"

Billy took aim with the Post-it and had another shot at the garbage can. This time the note went in and stayed in.

That's more like it.

Billy changed his posture and pivoted on one foot, transforming himself once again into a reporter.

"And what of Jim and Linda's son, Billy? How does *he* feel about all this?" Billy went on, clutching an imaginary microphone as he strode from the kitchen back to the living room. "Well, let's ask him. Billy, how *do* you feel about all this?"

"You want the truth?" said Billy, switching to his own voice. "I think it stinks. I think it's a lousy way to treat a devoted son who is so bright, well behaved, and good-looking."

Billy drew his eyebrows into an expression of great sympathy: he was the reporter again. "Tell me, Billy, do you think it *bothers* your parents that you have to spend so many evenings at home by yourself? Do you think they feel the least bit *guilty* that you have to eat takeout night after night rather than home-cooked meals? Indeed, do you suppose—as your parents dash madly from one skeeter gig to another—that they even *think* of you *at all*?"

Billy stopped, stood between the couch and the coffee table, and let out a long sigh. He dropped the imaginary microphone and the phony voice along with it.

"I don't know." Billy flopped onto the couch. "Probably not."

It hadn't been so bad the previous year, when Billy's best friend, Nathan Burns, was still living in Piffling. Nathan was the only kid at Piffling Elementary who was as obsessed with extreme sports as Billy was. They used to spend practically every weekend together, mountain-biking the cliffs that led down to the Piffling River, skateboarding across every handrail in town (they both had the scrapes, bruises, and occasional fractures to prove it), and even street luging on their homemade luges, which was apparently outlawed by some city ordinance or another. The only thing Billy and Nathan hadn't tried was sneaking a ride on the brand-new Harley-Davidson Nathan's father had stashed away in the garage.

They would have tried it eventually, for sure. But then Nathan's family moved to Los Angeles for his father's work. There were other kids at Piffling Elementary who were into extreme sports a little. They just weren't willing to risk life and limb the way Nathan was. Billy soon realized that finding a new best friend was going to take a while. In the meantime, it was looking like it would be THE USUAL for many months to come.

Piker, Billy's Scottish terrier, lifted her head from the recliner on the other side of the room, snorted, and went back to sleep.

BACK LATE, DON'T WAIT UP.

Billy had never been able to figure out why so much of his parents' work was done at night. Exterminators didn't normally work at night, did they? Were they trying to catch the bugs snoozing? Kids at school thought he was lucky. "If my parents left *me* alone at night like that," Nelson Skubblemeyer had said just the other day, "I'd be partyin' like nobody's business. I'd be, like, 'Yo, party tonight at my place. . . .' " (Nelson always said the word *party* as if it rhymed with *sauté*: in spite of his name, he'd somehow convinced himself he was the coolest kid in the sixth grade.)

Billy had never thrown a party while his parents were out on a skeeter gig. He wouldn't have been able to get away with it even if he'd tried. There was someone keeping an eye on him.

DRRIIIIIIINGG

Leo Krebs, thought Billy. *Right on schedule.* Billy normally didn't let the phone ring more than twice before answering. But when he was pretty sure it was Leo, the high school sophomore down the street who "looked after" him whenever his parents were gone at night, he had a policy of screening calls.

DRRIIIIIINGG

Billy leaned back into the couch and did his best Leo impersonation: "Dude. Pick up. I know you're there." Doing a good Leo meant breathing a lot of air into your voice and ending every sentence as if it were a question. Like Keanu Reeves, only more so.

DRRIIIIIINGG

Billy's voice had begun to change the previous summer, greatly increasing the range of impersonations he could do (which had been pretty impressive to begin with). "Duu-ude. You're wastin' my time here."

DRRIIIIIINGG

One more ring and the answering machine would kick in.

DRRIIIIIINGG

There was a *plick,* then a *jrrrr,* then: "Your pest problems are at an end . . . ," Jim Clikk's voice said. Billy jumped in and recited the words right along with the answering machine, creating the effect of two Jim Clikks speaking simultaneously. ". . . because you're seconds away from making an appointment with the extermination experts at BUGZ-B-GON. Just leave your name and number after the tone and we'll get back to you as soon as we can."

DWEEEEEP

"Dude." It was Leo, all right. "Pick up. I know you're there."

Billy grabbed the remote off the coffee table and clicked the television on. When dealing with one of Leo's check-in calls, it was essential to have every bit of audiovisual distraction available.

"Duu-ude. You're wastin' my time here."

Billy reached over, grabbed the cordless phone from one of the side tables, and pressed Talk.

"Leonard," he said, knowing how much Leo disliked being called by his full name. Well, at least he *hoped* Leo disliked it. Billy didn't exactly hate Leo, but he wasn't too crazy about him either. Part of it was Leo's *I'm older than you and don't forget it* attitude. Most of it, though, was Billy resenting the whole idea of being baby-sat at all. He was old enough to take care of himself.

"Dude," said Leo in return. He never called Billy anything other than dude. Leo probably called little old ladies dude. "Look, your folks told me they wouldn't be back until, like, midnight or whatever . . ."

Billy was remoting his way through a bunch of cartoon shows. He paused on an old low-budget monster movie.

". . . so I can either come over there and babysit you for a couple hours—which neither of us wants—or just check in again at ten and make sure you're still alive. Not that I want you to be."

"C'mon, Leonard. You don't want anything bad to happen to me. You'd be out twenty bucks a week."

Normally Billy would have come up with a better verbal jab than the twenty bucks line, but he was devoting most of his attention to the image on the television screen: an enormous creature with lobster claws going to great lengths to stomp his way into a cheap imitation of Disneyland. There didn't seem to be any special reason why. Maybe he'd run out of office buildings and power stations to wreck.

"All right, dude. Ten o'clock it is. Pick up the phone next time, will ya?"

"Okay, Leonard. And hey: tell your skater buddies to learn some new moves. My gramma can do better kickflips than that."

Billy shut off the phone with great relief. He knew that the money his parents paid Leo involved him physically being inside the Clikk home. Periodically Leo would skip the phone call and just arrive at the front door. On these occasions he always left behind some very clear proof that he'd been there—doodles on a notepad, a half-finished bottle of Gatorade—apparently thinking a bit of Leo-was-here evidence every once in a while would be enough to convince Billy's parents they weren't completely wasting their twenty dollars.

Doodles on notepads. Bottles of Gatorade. Billy noticed stuff like that: details. He'd always had a knack for it, even when he was just a kindergartner. If the dark blue crayon in Crayola's big box went from being called cerulean one year to cornflower the next, Billy knew about it and had a preference. And it wasn't just kid stuff. If Billy got even half a second's glance under the hood of a Hummer H2, he could tell which parts were new, which were old, and which parts the shady repairman had used strictly to skim money off the bill.

The lobster creature had reached the roller-coaster mountain in the middle of the amusement park and was tearing apart its papier-mâché walls. Sweaty actors with loosened neckties pointed and screamed convincingly.

Man. This is one stupid movie. If I were fighting a monster like that, I'd just pull the zipper on his back, stick my head inside, and tell him to get a better costume.

Billy punched the remote and jumped from channel 63 to 64. The Shopping Network: two middle-aged women going nuts over a very ugly piece of jewelry. Punch, punch, punch, punch: 65, 66, 67, 68. Boring, boring, boring, and boring. He was just about to shut the television off.

Huh?

That guy on TV.

That guy looked an *awful* lot like his dad.

Billy sat up and leaned halfway over the coffee table, staring with all his might. Piker sat up too.

The TV screen was filled with unsteady handheld video: some kind of ticker-tape parade. Street signs in a foreign language, early-morning sunlight. Dark-haired people with open-necked shirts, shouting, cheering. And there, in a big convertible sailing slowly through the crowds . . .

That's Dad!

No, it can't be.

Billy pressed the VCR button on the remote and then hit Record.

Bee-beep, bee-beep, bee-beep

"No tape!" Billy jumped off the couch, leaped over the coffee table, and fumbled for a blank videotape from the shelf under the TV, all the while keeping his eyes glued to the screen. Piker jumped down from the chair and began whining loudly.

"That can't be him," said Billy. "It's impossible."

Billy's heart was beating faster. He tore the cellophane off the videotape and crammed it into the VCR as quickly as he could. He punched the Record button and sat down on the coffee table to continue watching the program.

"That's not Dad. It just . . . can't be. This stuff was obviously shot in a foreign country. Dad never goes to other countries. Except, like, Canada."

But the man had the same face as Billy's father: the wide forehead, the slightly grayed wavy hair, the enormous protruding jaw. There was a woman seated next to him. It was hard to tell because she was wearing a wide-brimmed hat, but that was . . . Billy's mom, wasn't it? She had the same perky nose, the same thin-lipped mouth, and—from what he could see, anyway—was wearing the exact same style of thick-rimmed glasses.

No. Way.

Billy was now leaning so far forward that his face was no more than ten inches from the TV screen. He noticed something about the trees and buildings in the video: everything was dripping with some kind of thick, purplish liquid. As if kids had gone on a rampage with giant purple-yolked eggs.

What the heck is that stuff?

Piker barked once loudly.

A woman's voice accompanied the video, no doubt providing valuable information, but none of it was in English. A small icon in the lower right-hand corner of the TV screen confirmed what Billy already suspected: this was the International Channel, that weird cable station that went from Middle Eastern movies to Korean soap operas to Mexican news programs every half hour or so.

Billy trained his eyes on the pixelated faces before him. The camera zoomed in, went drastically out of focus, refocused on a palm tree, then finally brought the faces into some degree of detail. It *was* them. There could be no mistaking it. These were the same two people he'd eaten breakfast with, gone to monster truck shows with, and opened presents with every Christmas morning for the last twelve years.

The footage cut abruptly to a woman behind a desk reading the news. She had deeply tanned skin and almond-shaped eyes. Though she had yet to say a single word in English, Billy could tell by the way she paused and shuffled the papers in front of her that she was switching from one news story to another.

Billy was now off the coffee table and on his feet. He pressed Rewind and watched the video again. And again. And again. He memorized the details: the fruits in the market off to the side of the road (there were papayas, mangos, and bananas by the truckload), the make of the convertible (it was a black 1965 Lincoln Continental, in near-perfect condition), the footwear of the people in the crowd (sandals, one and all). He tried to decipher the words on street signs. One looked like it said DELA ROSA, another DELA COSTA.

This stuff was definitely *shot in a foreign country. My parents . . . are . . . in a foreign country.*

Billy rewound the tape for yet another viewing.

At least they have *been pretty recently, or else why would this be on a news show? It's morning where they are, nighttime here. This isn't just another country. They're on the other side of the freakin' planet here.*

SKEETER GIG. BACK LATE, DON'T WAIT UP.

Billy felt his knees buckle slightly, as if they were straining under the weight of not just his body but something else. Something heavier. Something much, much heavier.

"Skeeter gig?" said Billy. "*Skeeter* gig?"

A shiver ran down his spine and he swallowed hard.

"My parents didn't go on any skeeter gig. They . . . they *snuck off* somewhere . . . without *telling* me.

"Mom and Dad don't do stuff like this. It's, like, a major event with them when they cross the state line into Illinois. And now they're on the other side of the world? This is just *way* too weird to even be possible."

Then it hit him: he'd been tricked.

"Mom and Dad lied to me."

They were words he'd never had to say before.